A Taste For Blood

A Detective Johnny (One Eye) Hawke Novel

David Stuart Davies

Sparkling Books

British Library Cataloguing in Publication Data. A catalogue record for this book is available from the British Library.

2.0

BIC code: FH
ISBN: 978-1-907230-46-2

Printed in the United Kingdom by Berforts Information Press

@SparklingBooks

David Stuart Davies is the author of five novels featuring private detective hero, Johnny Hawke, and another five novels featuring Sherlock Holmes as well as several non-fiction books about the Baker Street detective including the movie volume ***Starring Sherlock Holmes.***

As well as being a committee member of the Crime Writers' Association, and editing their monthly magazine, ***Red Herrings,*** David is the general contributing editor for Wordsworth Editions Mystery & Supernatural series and a major contributor of introductions to the Collectors' Library classic editions.

By the same author

Johnny (One Eye) Hawke Detective:

Forests of the Night
Comes the Dark
Without Conscience
Requiem for a Dummy
The Darkness of Death

The Further Adventures of Sherlock Holmes:

Sherlock Holmes & The Hentzau Affair
The Scroll of the Dead
Shadow of the Rat
The Tangled Skein
The Veiled Detective

and many other titles

To Alanna Knight

A lovely lady who is both a good friend and an inspiration

A Taste For Blood

David Stuart Davies

PROLOGUE

He would never forget the blood. It wasn't just the quantity – although there was a great deal of it collected in dark, shining, sticky pools on the stone floor with errant rivulets escaping down the grooves between the flagstones. It wasn't just that sweet sickly smell either, which assailed his nostrils with pungent ferocity and etched itself forever on his memory, or the crimson stains splattered on the walls and floor that had remained with him, to return at the midnight hour to haunt his dreams. Most of all it was that face, that crazed visage with mad bulbous eyes and chomping teeth. Revisiting the scene in his nightmares, these images seem to shift and spread like a living organism coagulating into one great patch of red and then from the crimson mist the giant mouth would appear ready to swallow him up.

At this juncture, he would jerk himself awake with a brief tortured sigh, his body drenched in sweat. 'Just a silly nightmare,' he would murmur to placate his concerned wife Sheila and pat her shoulder reassuringly. 'Just a silly nightmare.'

Almost ten years later, the nightmares still came. Not as often but the images were still as vibrant, as threatening, as horrific as ever. He never talked about them to anyone, not even Sheila. They were his personal burdens and he was determined that they should remain so. He certainly didn't want to reveal his secret to his colleagues and have some brain doctor try to analyse his disturbed psyche. Besides if it got out that Detective Inspector David Llewellyn was being scared witless by bad dreams it would hardly do much for his police career. So, with typical stoical reserve, his 'silly nightmares' remained private and self contained.

Until…

ONE

1935

The night was bitterly cold and the frosty lawn shimmered like a silver carpet in the bright moonlight. Concealed in the shrubbery, Detective Sergeant David Llewellyn gazed at the dark and silent house some fifty yards away. His body was stiff with apprehension and fear while his bowels churned with nervous tension. He knew he shouldn't be here. He knew he was taking a risk. He knew he was following his heart rather than his head. But he also knew that sometimes one had to take risks to achieve the right result.

The house, Hawthorn Lodge, gothic and imposing, appeared as a black threatening silhouette against the lighter star-studded sky. It rose out of the earth like a giant claw, its gables and chimneys scratching the sky, while its windows glistened darkly in the moonlight. There was no observable sign of life or occupancy and yet Llewellyn knew that there was some one in there: Doctor Ralph Northcote.

No doubt he was in his basement, a section of the house that the doctor had successfully kept secret from the officers when they had searched the premises. What he was doing there? Llewellyn preferred not to think about it at that moment. His boss, Inspector Sharples, a whisker off retirement, was a tired and sloppy officer and had not been thorough or dogged enough in his investigations. Llewellyn had been sure that a house as large as Hawthorn Lodge would have quarters below ground – a wine and keeping cellar at least – but Sharples wasn't interested. He was convinced that the arrogant and smarmy Dr Ralph

Northcote was in no way associated with the terrible crimes he was investigating. How could a man of such intelligence, refinement and breeding perpetrate such horrible murders? The fiend who slaughtered those women was an animal, a beast, a creature of the gutter, not a respectable and respected medical man. Or so the blinkered, forelock tugging Inspector believed.

David Llewellyn had other ideas.

To satisfy his curiosity – at least – he had visited the local solicitor's office where he had been able to examine the original plans for Hawthorn Lodge. To his delight and satisfaction he had discovered that, as he suspected, the house did have a series of cellars. The plans indicated that these chambers were accessed by an entrance in the kitchen. However, instead of passing this information on to his superior, Llewellyn had decided to carry out some undercover work of his own. Why should he allow the old duffer Sharples take the credit for his detective prowess? He'd been sneered at and ridiculed when he'd offered his opinion, his strong conviction, that Dr Northcote was the man they were after.

Now he intended to prove it.

Gripping the police revolver in his pocket with one hand and picking up his battered canvas bag with the other, David Llewellyn emerged from the shrubbery and with a measured tread made his way across the lawn towards the front of the house, his footsteps leaving dark imprints in the frosted grass like the trail of some ghostly creature. On reaching one of the tall sitting-room windows, he knelt down in the flowerbed and withdrew a jemmy from the bag. With several deft movements, accompanied by the gentle sound of splintering wood, he managed to prise the window from its fastenings and open it a few inches. That was all that was needed. Gripping the lower edge of the window with both hands and exerting all his strength he pushed it higher, creating an aperture large enough to allow him to pass through.

Within moments he was in the house, a gentle smile of satisfaction resting on his taut features. From the innards of the bag, he extracted a torch. He had visited the house on two previous occasions in a formal and more conventional capacity with Sharples. These visits, allied to his studies of the plans, gave him the confidence to move swiftly through the dark sitting room, into the hallway and towards the kitchen.

* * *

The murders had started six months earlier. The pattern was the same in all four cases. A young woman in her early twenties was reported missing by her distraught parents and then a few days later her mutilated body was discovered in woodland or waste ground. In all instances the victim's arms, legs and breasts had been amputated and were missing. There was also evidence that the victim had been tortured. Most of the gruesome details had been held back from the press but despite that, because of the youth of the victims, the murderer had been labelled 'The Ghoul' by the more downmarket rags.

The limbs had been expertly severed and so it was suspected that a member of the medical profession was the perpetrator of these horrendous crimes. The girls had all lived within five miles of Hampstead Heath and doctors and surgeons residing within this radius had fallen under particular scrutiny. Two suspects emerged: Stanley Prince, a middle-aged GP who had been struck off the medical register some years before for conducting a series of abortions; and Ralph Northcote, a surgeon at St Luke's Hospital who twelve months earlier had been accused of assault by one of the nurses who had mysteriously disappeared before she could testify against him at a medical tribunal. As a result, the case was dropped and Northcote continued to practice.

Inspector Brian Sharples was placed in charge of the case and given one of the promising new live wires at the Yard, Detective Sergeant David Llewellyn, as his assistant. The two men did not get on. Sharples was an old hand, steady on the tiller, a great believer in doing things by the book, a book it seemed to Llewellyn that Sharples had written himself at some time back in the Middle Ages. With Sharples it was a case of softly, softly, catchee monkey. This may work in the long run, thought Llewellyn, but there may be three or four more murders before this particular monkey was apprehended. Llewellyn was a great believer in stirring up the waters and in the power of intuition. He was convinced that he had a nose for sniffing out a murderer.

Both Prince and Northcote were investigated and interviewed, but apart from their past misdemeanours nothing could be pinned on them. However, Llewellyn did not like Northcote. There was something about his oh-so-charming and rather slimy manner that set alarm bells ringing for the young Detective Sergeant. So much so that, unknown to Sharples, and any other of his colleagues, he had started to do a little digging on his own. Northcote was now in his mid-thirties and living alone, but in his youth he had been a bit of a ladies' man with, Llewellyn discovered, a string of broken engagements. Engagements which had all been ended by the girls. Llewellyn had managed to track one of these girls down and interview her. Doreen French was touching forty now, plump and comfortable looking. She had married a greengrocer and was the mother of twins. She seemed content with her lot and more than happy to talk about Northcote. She revealed nothing that was legally incriminating, but confirmed Llewellyn's impression that the man was odd and put up a false front to the world. 'In the end,' said Doreen French, her eyes twinkling brightly, 'he gave me the willies. He was… how can I say…? He liked to touch me. Not in a sexual way, you understand, but… just to touch my skin. He loved to run his fingers down my bare arm. He once gave my arm such a squeeze, it caused a great big bruise. He wasn't much of a kisser, but …' she giggled innocently… 'he did like to lick me. On my cheek and round the back of the neck. I thought it was sweet at first. Affectionate like – but in the end… as I say, it gave me the willies'.

Llewellyn nodded sympathetically. It would give him the willies too. 'Was he ever violent to you?'

Doreen did not have to ponder this one. 'Oh, no. Not deliberately, anyway. There was that bruise I mentioned, but he never slapped me or anything like that. But I have to say, that towards the end, I just didn't like being alone with him. He just seemed odd. What had started out as endearing quirks became rather spooky. And his eating habits… ugh!'

'What about them?'

'Well, he hardly ate anything that was cooked. He liked raw steak and his lamb chops hardly sat in the pan a minute before they were on his plate, all bloody and raw.' Doreen pulled a face that effectively mirrored her revulsion.

Well, thought David, there was nothing in the interview that would provide evidence that Northcote was this Ghoul, but he certainly seemed a strange chap and it was certainly a strange chap with medical knowledge who was murdering these young girls. Now a fifth one had disappeared. Her body had not been found yet so there was a slim chance that she was still alive. Very slim, he had to admit. Sharples had refused to interview Northcote again –

'We've nothing to go on, lad. We're here to investigate crimes not cause a nuisance to respectable law abiding folk.' And so David decided to take things into his own hands.

* * *

Once in the kitchen, he examined the walls carefully for some kind of hidden door that would provide access to the cellars. His search was fruitless, however. As he stood in the centre of the lofty chamber, the beam of his torch slowly scanning his surroundings, a sound came to his ears, one which froze his blood.

It was a high-pitched scream of pain. It was sharp and piercing like nails down a blackboard. He shuddered involuntarily at the sound. Where had it come from? It was clear yet distant, like a train whistle down a long tunnel. He listened, straining his ears in the hissing silence but the sound did not come again. As he waited in the dark, he relaxed the hold on his torch and the shaft of light sank towards the floor and rested on the base of a large kitchen cabinet by the far wall. What it illuminated made Llewellyn's heart skip a beat. There were faint skid marks marking the dark wooden flooring: tiny groves that had imprinted themselves on the boards. It was quite clear to Llewellyn that these had been made by the stout legs of the cabinet as it had been pulled away from the wall.

With a tight grin, he rested the torch on the large kitchen table in the centre of the room so that the beam fell on to the cabinet and then he attempted to drag it away from the wall. Kneeling in order to obtain a more secure purchase, he tugged hard at the lower section. Slowly the cabinet moved, the feet following exactly the track of the grooves in the floor. When he had managed to create a gap between the wall and the cabinet big enough for him to squeeze himself into, he saw it.

Llewellyn's grin broadened. 'The secret door,' he

whispered to himself.

He now pushed the cabinet fully clear of the wall and attempted to open the door. The handle rattled encouragingly but the door did not budge. It was locked. This did not daunt Llewellyn for although the lock was new and stout, the door was old. Retrieving the jemmy from his canvas bag, he got to work levering the door open. It was the work of a matter of moments. The wood splintered easily and surrendered to the force of the jemmy.

Gingerly he pulled the door open and with the aid of his torch he peered into the darkness beyond. There was a set of stone steps leading down into ebony void. 'Now the adventure really starts,' he muttered to himself as he moved slowly forward into the cold blackness. On reaching the bottom of the stairs he thought he heard faint, indistinguishable noises in the distance. How far away they were he could not tell. Maybe it was just the movement of rats and mice – maybe it was something else. Using his torch like a searchlight, he tried to get a sense of his surroundings. He was in a passageway with a low vaulted ceiling. He saw that there were two light bulbs dangling down but no sign of a switch by which to turn them on. He knew, however, that it would be foolish to do so even if he could. He had no intention of announcing his presence in such an ostentatious fashion.

On reaching the end of the passage, he came to another door. A thin line of light seeped out at its base. This is it, thought Llewellyn, heart thumping. Swiftly he clicked off the torch and stowed it away in his coat pocket and then pulled out his revolver before turning the handle of the door. This one was not locked. Gently he opened it and stepped inside. The first impression was of the brightness of the chamber. The walls and floor were covered in white ceramic tiles while fierce strip lights hung down from the ceiling flooding the room with harsh illumination which created dense shadows. It had the antiseptic ambience of an operating theatre.

An operating theatre.

In the centre of the room was a stone slab on which was laid the twitching naked body of a young girl. At first glance, she seemed to be coated from head to foot in some dark shiny substance. Then, to Llewellyn's horror, he realised that it was blood. Leaning over her was a man in a white coat which was also splattered with crimson stains. As Llewellyn entered the chamber the man glanced up in surprise, his eyes wide and manic. It was a moment that was forever etched on David's mind. Like a scar, that image was to stay with him for life; it was seared into his consciousness ready to feed his nightmares and catch him unawares during unsuspecting waking moments. It was as though a fierce flashbulb had exploded, the harsh, vibrant light freezing the scene as vile photograph.

The creature seemed unconcerned that he had been disturbed in his activity. The lower half of his face was dripping with blood and something seemed to be trailing from his mouth, glistening and moist. As Llewellyn took a step nearer, he realised to his disgust that it was a piece of pink meat. Instinctively, his gaze moved to the mutilated body of the naked girl and then the truth hit him like a mighty blow to the solar plexus. This fiend was eating her flesh.

TWO

1944

After the death of my girlfriend Max… after her brutal murder… I spiralled down into an undignified state of self-pity. I tried to escape reality through booze and sleep, failing to function either as a detective or even a human being. I rejected the ministerings and comfort offered by those close to me: Peter, my sort-of adopted son, Benny, the little Jewish café owner who treated me like family, and my old mate Detective Inspector David Llewellyn. In their various ways they all tried to shake me out of my depressive malaise, but failed. It was not their fault. Perversely, I didn't want to be shaken. I wanted to wallow. Ironically, as I think back to that period now, I can see that being deeply miserable was in a strange way the only thing that was keeping me sane.

As an orphan, I had never seen much affection in my life and then to meet the beautiful Max and receive it from her in spades was miraculous and wonderful. My innate cynicism forged out of a life of disappointments should have warned me that it wouldn't last, but nothing or no one could have prepared me for the savage and dramatic way in which she would be taken from me. What increased my pain was the sense of guilt I felt for her death. She was killed by a crazed maniac as a means of wreaking revenge on me.* She was an innocent who had wandered into my dirty little world and because of me she had lost her life. It was my fault that she ended up with a bullet in her head.

* *See* ***The Darkness of Death****, the fifth Johnny One Eye novel, for full details*

My fault.

The image of my dead love with her wide staring eyes and the spidery tendrils of blood spilling down her face haunted me in those months and days that followed. And, indeed, haunt me still.

What dragged me back to reality and, in truth, saved my sanity was one of the strangest and most challenging episodes of my life. It was late March and winter's grip on the country was still in evidence. It might have been spring on the calendar, but the elements were not acknowledging the fact. The daffodils and crocus may have reluctantly raised their heads about the stiff frost-bound earth, but the fierce gales continued to blow and sleet showers doused the city. It was on such a foul morning when the wind rattled the window panes and the rain sloshed against the glass that I was sitting huddled by the electric fire, clasping a cup of hot coffee while trying to raise some enthusiasm for facing the day. I realised that I had to go back to work and soon. I had been scrounging on my savings such as they were for the last few months and as a result they had dwindled drastically and were now in danger of disappearing altogether. I had turned down a couple of mundane cases simply because I couldn't face the prospect of returning to my old routine, pretending that everything was normal again. 'Pull yourself together man', would be the sentiment. 'What the hell, life goes on y'know!' Sorry, but I just couldn't accept that resilient and unfeeling philosophy.

However, as I sat in my cramped sitting room, staring at the small twisted orange wires of the electric fire gently vibrating with feeble warmth I came to accept that even mundane cases pay and I needed money. Even if I was just going to spend it on booze. I knew that it really was time to try and get back in the saddle as that stupid phrase has it. I could hear Benny's voice in my head: 'Work is the best antidote to sorrow, my boy.' Well, perhaps the old boy was right.

With some effort, I dragged myself down the hall to the bathroom. I gazed at myself in the mirror over the sink. It was probably the first time I really had looked at myself properly since before Max died. I was shocked by what I saw. Here was a stranger. A grey, hollow-cheeked ghost of a man, wearing a haggard parody of my face, was staring back at me. My vivid impersonation of a consumptive tramp was enhanced by the several days' growth of beard.

Suddenly I heard another voice inside my head. This time it was my own and surprisingly, shockingly, it came up with a new thought – something that had not crossed my mind until the image of the dissipated wreck in the mirror had prompted it. What would Max think? I asked myself. Would she be happy at the way you are behaving? Of course not. She wouldn't want you this way, would she? Not her Johnny. By turning into a self-pitying drunk I was letting her down. This realisation struck me hard. What a stupid bastard I was!

With some effort, I held back a sob and rooted in my toilet bag for my razor. 'Let's get rid of the fuzz for a start' I muttered to myself through gritted teeth.

Thirty minutes later, I was back in my sitting room fully dressed with a clean white shirt on and a smooth chin and combed hair. I still looked like death warmed up, but a much tidier version than before. As I checked myself out in the mirror I even afforded myself a smile. It was a stranger to my face and it had difficulty settling there but I persevered and made it stay for a few seconds before it slipped away into the ether. Perhaps I was only pretending to myself that I could do this but, I reckoned, if I stuck to the pretence maybe that would become its own reality. I'd just got to try.

As a reward for all my efforts, I sank in my armchair and lit a cigarette. Watching the bluish smoke spiral gently away from the amber tip, I made plans for my day.

My first port of call was St Saviour's Church, the little Catholic church situated in one of the thoroughfares off the Edgware Road. It was here where Max was buried. I managed to buy a limp bunch of daffodils to place on her grave. The rain had stopped, but dark clouds loured over me and the wind stabbed me and pinched my nose as I stood in the graveyard and had a brief conversation with my dead love. 'I'm back,' I said. 'Back as me. Back as you knew me. Well, almost. I still don't have that spring in my step but I'm going to try, my love. I'm going to try for you. Be the old Johnny Hawke I used to be. I'll never quite manage that, but... I'll try to make you proud of me.' I grinned and dabbed my moist eye.

As I turned to go I was conscious of someone standing close to me. It was Father Sanderson, the priest who had conducted Max's funeral and had been so kind and understanding towards me.

'Hello, Johnny,' he said, his blue eyes twinkling. 'How are you?'

I gave a gentle shrug. 'I think I'm on the mend.'

'That's good to hear. The pain of loss never quite goes away, nor should it, but it does become easier to bear. It's early days yet.'

I nodded.

'I wonder if I could have a word with you. I have a little problem you may be able to help me with.'

'Well, yes, of course, if you think I can be of any use.'

'How about a cup of tea and a digestive biscuit in my office? That should help warm you up. I must admit you look like a frozen ghost.'

I grinned. 'I'm anybody's for a cuppa and a biscuit.'

* * *

Father Sanderson's office was a cramped little chamber just beyond the vestry. It smelled of damp, dust and altar candles. Various tomes were piled up along the walls and there were a couple of bentwood chairs and a bench which also held books as well as a gas ring, kettle and other tea-making equipment. Alongside these were several goblets and a bottle of what I assumed was communion wine standing on an old newspaper. Around the base of the bottle, the paper was spotted with dried splashes of the wine, creating a delicate pattern in varying hues of red.

'Sit yourself down, Johnny, and I'll brew up.'

I did as he asked, wrapping my overcoat around me. For my money it was colder in here that it was outside in the graveyard. A few minutes later I was sipping a cup of scalding hot tea and nibbling on a damp digestive.

'Sorry to bother you, but I'm in a bit of a quandary, really,' said the old cleric as he seated himself opposite me. He had a kind, heavily wrinkled face framed by a thatch of thick white hair. I guessed that he was in his seventies, but he could have been younger: it was just that his desiccated skin and stooped shoulders suggested otherwise.

'I know you are a kind of detective, Johnny, and I thought you might be able to offer me some advice,' he began hesitantly. It was obvious that he felt awkward about having to approach me in this way.

'If I can,' I said. 'What's the problem?'

'It's one of my parishioners, Annie Salter. She's a widow. A lady in her fifties. Lost a son at Dunkirk. Been a regular at St Saviour's for many a year. A few weeks ago I found her in the church. She was praying in one of the pews near the altar and seemed upset. She was muttering something. I could not hear the words but it was quite clear that she was asking for help – for divine assistance. I stood in the shadows not wanting to interrupt her private moment. From time to time she would pause in order to stifle a sob and then she would begin again. My heart went out to the poor soul. Whatever afflicted her, it was tearing her apart.

'I waited at the back of the church while she had finished and then as she made to leave I approached her. I could see clearly that she'd been crying – and I thought I might be able to help her. Offer comfort, at least.'

'What is troubling you, my dear?' I asked, taking her hands in mine.

She tried to shrug off her distress with a faint smile. 'I'm all right, really. Just feeling a little low. Came in to ask Jesus for some help. It's the war, isn't it? Sometimes it gets you down a bit.'

I knew that she was not telling me the truth. Not the full story, at least. I told her that I was there to listen, to help. I was one of Jesus's helpers. Perhaps I could come to her aid. My offer of help seemed to upset her more than ever.

'At the moment, I don't think anyone can help me,' she told me as her eyes moistened again. Then she pulled her hands from mine and hurried away without further words or a backward glance.

'That was the last time I saw her.'

I said nothing. I knew that there was more to come. There had to be.

'The following Sunday, Annie did not turn up for the Sunday service. I had not known her to miss in three years, apart from one occasion when she was struck down with influenza. The following morning, I went round to her house to see if she was ill and needed some help. There was no reply when I knocked on the door. I knocked hard, I can tell you, Johnny.' He smiled. 'A priest always does. Sometimes the householder will hide behind the door hoping I'll go away. If you bang loud enough, eventually guilt makes them open up.' His smile broadened and then faded quickly. 'But on this occasion there was no reply. I was just about to leave when the lady next door popped her head over her threshold. 'I've not seen her since Friday. I reckon she might have gone away,' she said. 'Where to?' I asked and received a puzzled shrug in response.

'Annie's behaviour in church and her absence prayed on my mind. I was worried about her – so much so that I visited the house again the following Thursday. Still there was no reply. My concern grew. I thought it was time to take further action so I went down to the local bobby shop on Frampton Street. They know me down there and took my concerns seriously. Sergeant Harmsworth came back to the house with me and after the rigmarole of knocking and waiting, waiting but no response, he applied his weight to the door and forced it open. 'It'll be up to you, Father, to pay for any repairs,' he said trying to lighten the mood of the operation. We stood on the threshold and he called out Annie's name. His voice echoed through the innards of the house but no one answered. I feared the worst. And so did Sergeant Harmsworth if his grim features were anything to go by. We moved into the tiny hallway and then into the kitchen. All was neat and tidy. All perfectly normal, I suppose. And then we came into the living room. It was terrible, Johnny. Simply terrible. There she was dangling from one of the beams, her mouth agape, tongue sticking out, her eyes… her eyes… well, it was terrible.'

'She'd hung herself.'

Father Sanderson shot me a glance. 'Well, that's what it looked like. There was a dressing gown cord tied around her neck and a stool on its side under her. And there was a note on the mantelpiece.'

'What did it say?'

'I can tell you exactly what it said. Just five words only. 'I just couldn't go on.'

'A fairly traditional sentiment for a suicide.'

'Mmm. Exactly. Traditional. Cliché even. Oh, the police are quite convinced that poor Annie committed suicide.' He paused and flashed me a piercing glance.

'But you're not,' I said.

'No, I'm not. It's not her way. She was far more stoical than that. She's not a quitter. And another thing... that note. It's not her writing.'

'You told the police this.'

'Of course I did. They just said that when a person is in a disturbed phase of mind their handwriting goes haywire. They can't control their movements or some such notion. But I know, Johnny, I know that Annie did not write that note. Apart from the writing, it was too brief and trite for Annie.'

'What are you saying?' I asked, fairly certain I knew the answer anyway.

Father Sanderson looked me in the eye and said sternly, 'I am saying that she was murdered.'

THREE

Dr Francis Sexton sat in his car and stared through the windscreen at the forbidding building before him. Even on a bright day in March when the sky was making every effort to shrug off the greyness of winter and allow little patches of blue to appear, Newfield House looked bleak and gloomy. To Sexton the building, stark against the bright sky with drab stonework marked with the strands of long-dead ivy, and the strange acute angles of the gables, along with the blank shuttered windows, made the place look like an illustration from a work by Edgar Allan Poe – *The Fall of the House of Usher* – maybe. The house, an early Victorian monstrosity, stood in isolation in its own grounds, now uncared for and neglected, like the inmates within.

Sexton shifted his gaze to the paint-peeling notice erected near the main door:

Newfield House
Psychiatric Hospital
No Unauthorised Admittance
Home Office Property

Newfield House, once the house of some rich industrialist, had been converted to a lunatic asylum for the criminally insane as an overflow of Broadmoor and had only been renamed within the last ten years. The name may have changed but the purpose and régime remained more or less as it always had. There was little psychiatry practised there. It was just a matter of keeping the inmates contained and sedated. The state had seen fit not to hang them, so instead they must rot in a drug-induced state in this God forsaken place near the Essex marshes. Sexton could understand and to some extent sympathise with these sentiments. The twenty inmates had all committed horrendous crimes while 'the balance of their mind was affected.' Madmen, then. But as Sexton knew, madmen could also be rational and reasonable for most of the time. It should be possible to rehabilitate these creatures so they could return to society. They did not ask to be mad – just as a man who is deaf or blind or a fellow with a lisp did not ask for these disabilities. Madness was a disability. It was Fate or God who allowed it. It was up to man to help, not to condemn. That, at least, was the litany that Dr Francis Sexton preached and that is why the authorities with great reluctance allowed him to attend one of the inmates at Newfield for 'research purposes'. Sexton was writing a book on the human psyche with particular attention to the diseased criminal brain. That is what the authorities believed and that is why they permitted Dr Francis Sexton to visit Newfield the third Thursday in every month to spend time with one of its notorious inmates: Ralph Northcote.

* * *

The said inmate Dr Ralph Northcote waited for his visitor in a small, featureless room that had become his home for the last eight years. His cell, in fact. It consisted of a bed – clamped to the floor so that it could not be moved – a chair, a washbasin, and a small bookshelf crammed with medical volumes he had managed to retain from his old life and a barred window which was too high for him to peer out of, even if he stood on the chair, which he had no inclination to do. Northcote was no longer the lithe, clean-shaven charmer of his younger days. Not being able to shave unless under strict supervision, he had grown a straggly beard while boredom had led him to consume as much of the foul institutionalised food as he could. He was now a rotund, heavily bearded, blotchy-faced parody of his former self, looking much older than his forty-eight years. He certainly no longer resembled the man who had stood in the dock accused of a series of horrendous crimes. The man the press named as 'The Ghoul'.

Northcote was particularly excited about today's visit from his new friend, Francis. His monthly visits had become the highlight of his life in this dreary place. They thought him mad and that's why they had dumped him in this hellhole, to be forgotten, to rot until death. He wished they had hanged him. That, at least, would have been the end of it. He was not mad. He had known what he was doing. He would do it again – given half the chance. His passion for raw flesh may seem strange to the outside world, but to him it was no different from stuffing your face with bits of dead cow, pig or chicken. He was convinced that it was because of this fact that the judge hadn't dared to pass the death sentence. The old fool knew he was not mad but couldn't condemn him for his unusual appetite.

At first he had resented Francis Sexton's visits. He only agreed to them because they would bring some kind of novelty to his drab routine. But he didn't want to be scrutinised, analysed, compartmentalised and patronised. However, he soon realised that Francis would do none of these things. He had come in a spirit of friendship. Of course, he asked questions – wanted to know things about him, his history, his thoughts, what made him tick. But friends did that. And they had become friends. He knew that Francis grew to value these visits as much as he did. Northcote believed that a bond had grown between them and that was because Francis really understood him and his predilection.

Francis was the only one who had really listened to him, listened and understood his passion. He felt at ease with this man and was able to tell him things he had never confided to anyone else. Things about his childhood and his first encounter with uncooked flesh and the revelations that this had brought about. Francis never condemned or criticised him. Indeed, he began to smuggle in little treats: a piece of liver, a small cut of beef, and some pork. All uncooked and red with blood. It was their little secret. A secret that bonded them even closer.

And then the plan had developed. An idle remark. A casual aside. But it had created a spark with gradually ignited and the plan flickered into life.

And today was the day to put it into operation.

Through an innate ability to master his emotions, and a learned facility developed from being shut away in this Godforsaken dump, Northcote was able to maintain a cool and collected outlook even when exciting and dangerous things were about to happen. As he sat in his cell patiently waiting for the arrival of his visitor, the observer would have noticed nothing about his appearance to suggest a mood of suppressed anticipation and excitement. Except perhaps for the gentle – ever so gentle – movement of Northcote's thumbs. While all other parts of his body remain statue-like still, his thumbs circled each outer in a lazy moribund fashion. It was the one chink in his armour, his one expression of inner excitement. Meanwhile the eyes were dead, glacial and dead, and the body remained rigid with the feet splayed flat on the floor. You could hardly tell the man was breathing.

But the thumbs continued to move like comatose butterflies.

* * *

As was his usual practice, Dr Francis Sexton kept on his hat, scarf and coat once he was inside the building. He was such a regular visitor to Newfield that he only had to flash his authorisation in a casual fashion to the guard on reception before he was allowed to pass through the locked section into the hospital.

'You here again?' asked the guard in a cheery fashion, hardly looking up from his library book, a western with the title 'Me, Outlaw'.

Sexton nodded.

'Hardly seems five minutes since the last visit.' The man chuckled. 'Time flies when you're having fun.' He chuckled again at his own sarcasm and returned to the dust of Arizona.

Sexton made his way to E block where Northcote's cell was situated. It was a cold, gloomy building with the smell of damp and decay always in the air. The décor was a mixture of the faded and neglected original Victorian furnishings and the utilitarian touches institutionalised grimness. He passed a few staff on his way but no one took much notice of him or gave him a greeting.

Eventually he reached E block and passed through swing doors which led him down a short tiled corridor at the end of which was Northcote's cell: E 2. A young man in a white coat sat outside the room. It looked to Sexton as though he had dropped off to sleep – and who could blame him, sitting on guard outside a madman's room just in case he became unruly, agitated, violent. To Sexton's knowledge, Northcote had exhibited none of these symptoms since he had been admitted eight years ago. The sound of Sexton's shoes clipping sharply on the tiled floor seemed to rouse the young man from his doze. He glanced up and observed the approaching visitor. Before the doctor was upon him, he recognised that grey overcoat and the black fedora. He rose to his feet and taking a key from the pocket of his white coat he slipped it into the door.

'A glutton for punishment, I reckon that's what you are,' grinned the young man sleepily.

Sexton emitted a non-committal grunt.

The door swung open and he entered the cell. No sooner had he done so than the door clanged to behind him.

Northcote rose from his chair and the two men stood facing each other, neither of them opening their mouths, but their eyes spoke volumes. Gradually Northcote raised his right arm, and extended it towards his visitor. Sexton took it and the two men shook hands.

'Dr Sexton, it is so good to see you,' said Northcote in his strange gravelly voice, which had developed since his incarceration. He spoke little, hardly a few sentences a day, and it was as though his vocal chords had become rusty and were in danger of seizing up.

'And you too, Ralph,' he said with a ghost of a smile, as he placed his briefcase on the floor.

Northcote's eyes darted in its direction, wide with anticipation. 'You have perhaps brought me some treats.'

'Later. For now, it is time to get rid of that beard.'

Opening the briefcase he extracted a small cardboard box and handed it to Northcote. It contained a pair of scissors, a shaving brush and a piece of shaving soap. 'Put the debris in the box,' said Sexton.

Moving to the little sink with a piece of aluminium which acted as a mirror, he began chopping away at his unruly growth. Sexton, took off his hat, coat and scarf and sat on the bed to watch. Ten minutes later, Northcote had completed his task. Scratching his chin, he turned to his visitor. 'Well, what do you think?'

'Well, you look like the ghost of Christmas Past, but at least you don't look like you did.'

'Feels strange,' Northcote said, rubbing his chin. 'But that's good. Anything which has a touch of novelty is good in this place. Now, can I have my little treats?'

Sexton nodded and retrieved a small damp brown bag

from his briefcase. 'A little liver,' he said. 'Fresh meat is very hard to come by at this time,'

'The war, you mean?'

'Yes, the war.'

Northcote shook his head. 'I know nothing of the war in this shabby cocoon.' He tore open the bag and his eyes flickered with glee at the sight of the slimy red offal. There were two pieces each about the size of a child's hand. He snatched one up and slapped it to his mouth and chewing on it noisily for a few seconds, sucking the blood from it, before he bit into it. He gave a gurgle of delight as he chomped on a ragged fragment. Sexton watched with fascination as with the serious deliberation of an animal Northcote devoured the liver, slowly but with enthusiastic relish. When he had finished his lips and cheeks were smeared red. He looked like a crazy clown.

'You'd better clean your face,' said Sexton with a half smile.

'A little water clears us of this deed,' replied Northcote moving to the sink where he ran the tap and swilled the blood away. He stared as blood, now pink diluted by the water, spiralled away down the plughole.

'Thank you,' he said. 'That was most tasty. I get nothing like that in here. Everything is incinerated before it reaches a plate.'

Sexton ignored the remark. He had heard many similar ones before. It was Northcote's usual and predictable mantra after consuming his meaty titbit.

'Are you ready? Are you prepared?'

Northcote nodded. 'I am.'

* * *

The young man was interrupted from his day dream – a languorous affair that featured one of his favourite film stars in a state of undress – by a tapping on the door of cell

E 2.

'My session is over. I'm ready to leave now. Thank you,' said a voice.

It was exactly the same set of words Dr Sexton used on every occasion he visited.

The young man roused himself and unlocked the cell.

'Thank you,' said Sexton gruffly, pulling down his hat and then hurrying off along the corridor.

Some minutes later, he passed the guard on reception with a brief wave and was soon out into the growing dusk, breathing the free fresh air for the first time in eight years.

* * *

The evening meal, if such a grand term could be used for the lukewarm slop that was usually served up for the inmates of Newfield, was dished up at around six in the evening. And so it was on this occasion. The young man, still on duty, was presented with a tray by one of the kitchen staff. It contained a plate of mashed potatoes and some greyish meat substitute and piece of bread and a glass of water.

'For his lordship,' said the skivvy with a sneer.

The young man grinned and unlocked the cell door.

'Grub up,' he called as he entered. What met his eyes caused him to drop the tray. It clattered noisily on the tiled floor, the food spilling widely, some of it onto the trousers of the prone figure which was slumped face downwards by the bed.

The young man bent down and turned him over. The sight that met his eyes caused him to emit a strange strangled cry.

The unconscious face belonged to Dr Francis Sexton. He had a deep cut to his forehead which was seeping blood down his face.

'My God!' cried the young man. 'Christ!' he added for

good measure.

For a moment these exclamations were all he felt capable of. He was shocked and stunned into inaction by this weird turn of events. Gradually, his brain began to function and the situation before him came into focus. He rose to his feet and rushed into the corridor to press the alarm bell.

Out in the darkened car park, the man in Dr Francis Sexton's coat and hat unlocked the boot of his car and clambered inside.

FOUR

I sat staring at the pint of beer before me, watching the minute bubbles that were clinging to the rim of the glass disappear one by one. Fascinating though this vision was, my thoughts were elsewhere. I was running my interview with Father Sanderson over again in my mind. It was now lunchtime and I had sought shelter and sustenance – a pint and a cheese sandwich – in a small pub near the church.

The conversation – the one about the hanged woman whom Sanderson thought had been murdered – intrigued me as a detective. He was so convinced that the police had got it wrong, read the signs incorrectly and/or were happy to tidy up yet another death into the solved drawer. Well, it wouldn't be the first time this had happened. I was a copper before the war and I knew how desperate some officers were to wrap up an investigation as soon as possible and in a self imposed, blinkered fashion, accepting the probable as the truth rather than consider other options.

'I'd rather like you to investigate the matter, Johnny. Something is rotten in the state of Denmark, I'm afraid.'

'I'm not sure I'm the man to do the job,' I said, my feet already getting cold. I wasn't confident that I was up to this investigation and besides…

'Oh, I expect this to be a professional arrangement. I will pay you, of course.'

I shook my head vigorously. 'I couldn't accept money from you…'

'Because I'm a priest? A man of the cloth?'

My expression must have told him that he was correct in his assumption. How could I charge this impoverished old cleric for my services? And yet how could I afford the time and expenses to carry out an investigation for him? I was impoverished too.

'But I'm your client,' he responded with some warmth, his cheeks flushing. 'I have a little money put away for a rainy day and I reckon this is it. I was very fond of Annie. I wish to engage your services. This is not a favour I'm asking: I want to see justice done.'

Reluctantly I agreed, but I had little needles of guilt pricking me at the idea of taking money from the old fellow.

So that was it. My first case in the new year. My first case since the death of Max. I raised my glass of the now rather flat beer in a toast to the beginning of the rehabilitation of John Hawke.

While I was in the vicinity, I visited the police station on Frampton Street and as luck would have it, Sergeant Harmsworth was on desk duty. I explained who I was and Father Sanderson's concerns. Harmsworth grinned. He seemed an affable, comfortable chap, easy going if a little bovine. Unlike some coppers, he did not seem at all concerned that I was a private detective meddling in their affairs.

'Oh, I know all about the Father's theory that the old bird was murdered. I suppose being a man of God, he likes a little mystery. But I can tell you, there was nothing mysterious about Annie Salter's death. She hung herself. Plain and simple. There was not a scrap of evidence that a second party was involved. She even left a note.'

I nodded sympathetically to create the impression that I agreed with him fully and that Father Sanderson's notions were groundless.

'Could I see the note?' I asked.

'If we've still got it. Hang on. I'll have a look in the back office.'

He shifted his ample frame off his stool and disappeared into the far reaches of the station, returning a few minutes later holding a piece of paper.

'Here you are, Mr Hawke,' he grinned again, passing me the note. It was written in pencil on a scrap of paper torn from a cheap note book. There were the words as I had been told: 'I just can't go on any longer.' The handwriting was shaky and clumsy – whether this was as a result of emotion was a matter of contention.

'Father Sanderson says that this is not Annie Salter's handwriting,' I said casually.

Harmsworth shrugged. 'We'd nothing to judge it against, but as far as we could tell old Sanderson didn't have much familiarity with her writing in any case. And besides, if you are going to top yourself, the last thing you're gonna do is write in your best handwriting, are you? The hand'll be shaking too much for your actual copperplate.' He chuckled at his own conceit.

I turned the note over. The paper was blank but there was a little stain in the bottom corner.

'You can keep it if you like,' said Harmsworth, hoisting himself back on his stool. 'We've no use for it now.'

'Thank you,' I said graciously, slipping the note in my pocket. I reckoned I had seen more in that scrap of paper than the ample sergeant and his colleagues had.

My first real task was to find out more about Annie Salter: her history and her circumstances. Father Sanderson had been able to jot down the address of her cousin, a Mrs Frances Coulson, the only blood relative to attend the funeral. She lived in Chelmsford and her rather bijou semi-detached house was to be my first port of call.

If anything the day had grown more miserable by the time I had travelled to Chelmsford and found my way to Worthington Avenue. The sky had coagulated into a uniform dark grey and the wind had sharpened, piercing the folds of my overcoat causing me to shiver involuntarily.

Father Sanderson had told me that Frances Coulson was a woman in her mid-forties. She was a widow. Her husband had been something important in one of the city banks and had left her reasonably well provided for. That was all. I got the impression that he would have liked to tell me more about the woman, but he held back. No doubt he did not want to colour my impression of the lady. He thought I should make up my own mind about her. I was the detective after all. However, his reticence in this matter suggested to me that there was something he didn't quite like about Mrs Frances Coulson.

The Coulson dwelling was a very neat affair indeed: neat privet hedge, neat rectangular lawn, and neat shiny knocker on a neat green front door. I knocked, straightened my tie and waited.

I heard a voice somewhere in the house calling out, 'Coming.'

And indeed in less than a minute she came. Frances Coulson opened the door bringing with her a strong whiff of pungent perfume. When she saw me, the broad crimson grin disappeared almost immediately from her lips and her eyebrows lowered with disdain. I was either a great disappointment to her or she had been expecting someone else. I decided it was both.

'You're not selling anything, are you?' she said, managing to inject a sneer into the query.

I raised my hat and proffered my card. 'I'd like to have a little chat with you about Annie Salter,' I said gently with a polite smile.

She studied my card for a moment. 'Some detective you are,' she observed sourly, the sneer still in place. 'Haven't you heard? Annie Salter's dead.'

I nodded. 'Yes, I know. That's why I wanted a little chat with you.'

'What's this all about?'

'Well, if we can have that chat, I can explain.'

Indecision clouded her features for a moment and then she sighed. 'Very well, you'd better come in – but only for five minutes mind. I am expecting a visitor.'

That explained the crimson smile then.

Mrs Coulson was an attractive woman, full bodied, veering towards the stout with a smooth complexion which she attempted to hide with too much face powder. She wore a pin-striped pencil skirt and a tight angora sweater which emphasised her curves, which were substantial. At a little over five foot she was too short for my liking, but I can imagine many a middle-aged gent taking a fancy to the sweet-smelling and curvy Mrs C.

She lead me into the lounge, which like her was attractive, if a little over the top. Vibrant cushions, shiny trinkets and a garish rug clamoured for attention with the rather nauseous patterned wallpaper. There was a wedding photograph in a silver frame on the sideboard. It showed a younger but similarly over-dressed version of Mrs C with her husband outside a registrar office. She was in large checked suit with fox furs and a ridiculous hat; he, a weedy incongruous fellow, was draped in a pin striped suit that seemed two sizes two big for him and had a grin which suggested he couldn't believe how lucky he was to have this lovely creature on his arm and, indeed, in his bed.

The gramophone in the corner was playing a dance tune when we entered the room but, with quick staccato movements, Mrs C stopped it, replacing the lid with a sharp snap.

She didn't ask me to sit down or offer me a drink. She really did mean five minutes.

'What's all this about, then?' she snapped, standing with her back to the fireplace and giving me a gorgon stare.

'There is some concern… some doubt as to the manner of Annie's death and so…'

'Nonsense. She committed suicide. Didn't they find her hanging from her own ceiling? And she left a note.'

'The authenticity of the note has been called into question.'

'Authenticity? You mean whether she wrote it.'

I nodded. 'The handwriting…'

'She was distressed. She was just about to top herself. Her handwriting would have been all over the place…' She paused her eyes widening with feline ferocity. 'What are you suggesting?'

'It's possible that she didn't kill herself.'

She looked shocked at this suggestion. Whether she was acting, I couldn't tell. If she was, it was a good performance.

'You mean that she was… that someone killed her?'

I said nothing.

'That's ridiculous,' she said, reaching for a cigarette box on the mantelpiece. 'Who'd want to kill her? For what reason?'

'Sometimes there doesn't have to be a reason.'

There came that stare again. It almost came with a cat-like hiss this time.

'You're not with the police, are you?'

'No. My client is not satisfied with the suicide verdict. He's asked me to investigate.'

'Who is this lunatic, your client?'

'I'm not at liberty to say. It's a confidential matter, you understand.'

Frances Coulson rolled her eyes. 'Oh, I understand. Okay then, Dick Tracy, what do you want to know?'

'Anything you can tell me about Annie. You were

cousins.'

'We were cousins, yes, but in our case blood wasn't thicker than water. I knew her best when I was a kid and I didn't care much for her then. She was twelve years older than me and she used to look after me when mother went out.'

'Why didn't you like her?'

'She was too prim and proper. A real goody two shoes. She was no fun. And she remained no fun all her life. Hanging herself just about summed her up.'

'What do you know of her marriage? Her son?'

Suddenly Frances Coulson emitted a strange laugh. I guessed it was one of amusement but it was chilling in its sharpness and ferocity.

'What's so funny?' I ventured.

'That was when Madam Goody Two Shoes fell by the wayside. There was no marriage. The lady was no widow. She just got herself pregnant with the first man who showed any interest in her. And as soon as he'd got her into bed, he disappeared from sight and who could blame him. She invented the phantom hubby for the sake of respectability. Once the baby was born, she turned to religion and never let another man near her.'

'What about her son?'

'Malcolm? Don't know much about him. I only met him a couple of times. He could twist his mother round his little finger, though. Still, mustn't speak ill of the dead. Poor bugger copped it at Dunkirk. He was only nineteen.'

'When was the last time you saw Annie?'

'Oh, God, that was years ago... no, hang on a minute, I tell a lie. I bumped into her by accident a few months back when I was up in town. I was meeting a friend to go to the pictures and I'd just popped into Woolworth's down Oxford Street and when I came out I ran into Annie.'

'How did she seem?'

Frances Coulson shrugged. 'Much the same as always: dowdy and a bit miserable. No, actually she was more than a bit miserable. She seemed quite distracted. She didn't really want to talk, which was fine by me because we have... had... nothing in common. I mean blood ties stand for nothing, do they? There's more fallings out between families... Just because you're related doesn't mean you have to get on, have to like one another, does it? Anyway, I must admit I did feel a bit sorry for the poor old cow that last time. She seemed so down and ...old. She'd aged quite a bit. I suppose looking back, I can now see that she was probably depressed. Obviously she got worse and couldn't face going on anymore. And so...'

'Did she give any clues as to why she was depressed?'

'No. I asked her how life was treating her and she said something about God helping her to carry on.'

'What about friends? Do you know if she had any?'

'If she did, she never mentioned them to me. There might have been some sad soul at her church that she cottoned on to but somehow I doubt it. She was always a lonely woman, solitary, and when Malcolm died she shifted right back into her shell.' With a dramatic gesture she stubbed out her cigarette. 'If you want my advice, Mr Detective Man, I should abandon this wild goose chase. It's clear to me that Annie Salter committed suicide because she saw no reason to go on living. The idea of someone murdering her is plain daft. Why on earth would anyone want to? For what reason? How would her death benefit anyone? Forget it.'

She moved to the door and swung it open to indicate that the interview was over. That was OK by me. It was clear that I wouldn't be squeezing any more juice out of this particular orange. However, I was convinced she had told me all she wanted me to hear. That there was more to the story was certain, but I wouldn't get it from her.

'Thanks,' I said, heading through the hall to the outer door. 'You've been a great help.'

I could manipulate the truth also.

To be fair, the chat with the sparky Mrs Coulson hadn't been a complete waste of time. It did help me start to build up a picture, albeit one-sided at the moment, of the dead woman.

As I walked down the street, I passed a smart wiry fellow who seemed in a great hurry. He was the sort of chap one saw at the dog track: tweed jacket, bright yellow waistcoat, extremely shiny brogues and a trilby perched precariously on one side of his head. He had marked aquiline features but shifty with it. I suppose he was quite good looking if you go for that sort of thing. I reckoned Mrs Coulson did for I turned and watched his progress and saw that he moved swiftly up her garden path and rang the bell with alacrity. So, he was the reason I had only the five minutes.

* * *

On my way back into town, to my neck of the woods, I selected the information I thought was relevant and useful from my conversation with the prickly Mrs Coulson and filed it for further use. I reckoned that now I needed a more in depth chat with my client, Father Sanderson. At the moment he seemed to be the only person who could give me more unbiased details about Annie Salter's character and circumstances. Unbiased? Well, maybe I was being naïve.

Something the delectable Mrs Coulson had said was very pertinent to my investigation: 'How would her death benefit anyone?' The answer to that was the key to the whole matter. It usually boils down to motive. Why had Annie been killed? What purpose did her death serve? And to whom? That is what I had to discover. It was a challenge, but I had been faced with such challenges before and succeeded.

One thing I had realised in making my brief excursion to Chelmsford was that I had begun to feel a little bit like my old self again. It was good to be on the scent once more and exercising my detective skills, however modest. In fact I even managed a smile, a genuine one this time.

With this lightening of my mood, I decided that it was time to repair a few fences. It wasn't that I had fallen out with Benny, my old friend the café owner who had mother-henned me for years, it was that I had shunned him in recent months. I couldn't put up with his kindness and solace. I was hurting too much. I didn't want kind words and pots of tea. I was selfish, I suppose: I wanted to wallow unsolicited in my own grief.

It was growing dark when I reached his café. It was nearing closing time and there were just a couple of customers, each huddled over a cup of tea staring into space. Benny was at the counter reading a newspaper. He looked up as I entered, his face registering a mixture of emotions. It was clear that he didn't know whether he ought to be pleased or dismayed at my appearance.

'Any chance of tea and toast?' I said cheerily.

For a few moments Benny still remained uncertain how to react, so I broadened my grin. 'Today would be good.'

Benny's face suddenly lit up with pleasure. 'Today it is. Grab a seat and I'll have it with you in a trice.' With a little chuckle, he hurried off to the kitchen.

Five minutes later I was munching toast lavishly smothered with margarine and strawberry jam while Benny sat opposite me, an indulgent grin wreathing his features.

'So... how have you been?' he asked gently, testing the water.

'Miserable. Feeling sorry for myself, but I think I'm

starting to crawl out of that particular hole.'

'That's good. That's what we all want: the old Johnny back.'

'I'm not so sure you'll get that, but I'll try not to be a pain in the backside.'

Benny rolled his eyes. 'The old Johnny was always a pain in the backside.'

I nodded wearily. I reckoned that Benny was right.

Suddenly his features darkened. 'You should see Peter. He's been missing you. He comes in here twice a week and mopes. He's deliberately stayed away from you because he feels you don't want to see him…'

I shook my head with dismay. 'That's not true. It's just… it's just…'

Benny touched my arm. 'I know. But he's very young still. A tender shrub. Despite his height and long trousers, he's still just a kid and kids need love and affection.'

'What about the girlfriend? How's that going?'

'Oh, well, I think there has been some cooling off there.' He grinned. 'The flames of passion have waned a little. As I say he's still just a kid. He needs some mature advice.'

'I'm not sure I'm qualified to offer it. Look at the mess my life is in.'

'Hey, I thought we had stopped feeling sorry for ourself. Count your blessings, Mr Hawke. There are many folk in this town in a far worse state than you. You lost a loved one. Yes. But there are thousands out there in that same big boat. Remember with fondness and grieve for them but get on with your life. Grieve for them – not for yourself.'

As always, Benny was the source of sound advice.

FIVE

Gingerly Dr Sexton touched the bandages that covered the wounds on the back of his head.

'I reckon you'll have a stinker of a headache for quite a few days, sir' observed Inspector Horace Wisden gravely. He was a big man with a face like a rumpled pillow which housed a pair of kindly brown eyes.

'Yes. But I suppose I should be grateful that the brute didn't kill me.'

'Too true,' replied the inspector in a distracted fashion as he turned over the pages of his notebook.

They were sitting in a small office in Newfield House. It was here that Sexton had been bandaged by one of the medical orderlies after it had been established that he had suffered only surface wounds. He had then been interviewed by Wisden who had arrived on the scene with a body of men shortly after the alarm was given of Northcote's escape. The officers were searching the grounds while Sexton gave his statement.

'Well, I think we've got all the information that you can give us at the moment. It may be that we will call on you again, of course.'

'Does that mean I can go?'

'Well, yes, but are you sure you're safe to drive? I mean … a blow to the head.'

'Oh, I'm perfectly fine apart from the headache. I'm not likely to keel over at the wheel and I can see perfectly well. No double vision.'

Wisden seemed unconvinced. 'If you're sure.'

Sexton nodded gently. 'I'm sure.' He rose eagerly and made his way to the door but Wisden took hold of his sleeve and held him back. Sexton's heart skipped a beat.

'There was just one thing, sir.'

'Yes.' Sexton's voice was dry and tense.

'Well, I reckon you probably know this Northcote as well as anyone. The workings of his brain, I mean.'

Sexton gazed at the police inspector non-committally and said nothing.

'In your opinion, what is the fellow likely to do now that's he's out, escaped? Where do you think he will go? What will he do?'

'I am sorry but I can't really help you there. You see there's no logic in a mind like his. A mind without reason is unfathomable. We can sometimes discover what stimulates such violent and anti-social behaviour but one cannot predict what such a creature will do. It's a cliché, Inspector, but I'm afraid your guess is as good as mine.'

'Do you think he will try to kill again?'

Sexton gave a bleak smile. 'Oh, yes. I am quite sure of that.'

* * *

Dr Sexton stood on the steps by the main door of Newfield House and breathed in the cold night air. Already the frost was forming on the bushes and exposed rooftops of the outbuildings and his breath escaped in little white clouds. A number of police officers, their torches like mini-searchlights, were roaming the grounds in search of the fugitive.

It was a futile task.

Sexton made his way to his car. On reaching it, he tapped three times on the boot lid, paused and tapped three times again. After a brief pause, he heard the same set of taps repeated by the resident within the boot. Sexton beamed and swung himself into the driver's seat. Within minutes he had passed through the gates of the institution and was out on the open road.

* * *

Just over an hour later, he pulled into the drive of his detached house. Unlocking the garage, he drove the car inside and then closed the doors before pulling open the boot of the car. The occupant within, who had been hunched into a ball slowly unfurled himself with a groan. With the help of Sexton he managed to clamber out of the boot. With a further groan, he stood erect. For some moments neither man spoke.

Northcote eventually stretched, his arms reaching above his head and grinned. 'That feels good,' he said at length, almost to himself.

'Let's go into the house and get you settled in your quarters,' said Sexton with some eagerness. He was anxious to have the fugitive out of sight.

'Lead on,' replied Northcote easily. He was enjoying himself.

Once inside the house, Sexton drew the curtains in the sitting room before switching on the lights. Northcote slumped down in an arm chair, his feet splaying out before him. 'This is grand,' he said, still grinning. 'After what I've been used to it's like the Ritz.'

'A cup of tea or something stronger?'

'Tea will do just fine for now. I reckon I need to find my sea legs before I get onto the liquor with not having had a drop for eight years.'

'O.K. I won't be a moment. Then we can talk.' Sexton bustled off into the kitchen.

Left alone Northcote sat back, closed his eyes and relaxed. He couldn't remember the last time he felt so contented. He could hear the rattling of tea cups and the gush of water into the kettle and the popping of the gas ring in the kitchen – ordinary domestic noises that were music to his ears. He had almost fallen asleep by the time Sexton returned with a tea tray.

The tea was dark brown and strong. Northcote gulped it down. 'Not your normal brew, is it?'

'Earl Grey. Very refreshing. Would you care for another cup?'

'Yes, I think I will.'

Sexton poured him another cup. He himself had settled for a gin and tonic.

'Smooth as a baby's bottom, eh?' said Northcote as he sipped his second cup of tea, his voice heavy and tired.

Sexton nodded. Automatically his fingers reached for his bandaged scalp. As he pressed gently, he felt a small twinge of pain. 'You certainly gave me a bit of a headache,' he observed drily. There was no humour in his voice.

Northcote gave a lazy grin. 'Sorry about that but we needed some authenticity.'

He stumbled over the word 'authenticity' and shook his head slowly as if to dislodge the overpowering sensation of tiredness that was creeping over him. It was as if all the life in his body was being drained from him.

'Authenticity,' he repeated in the same clumsy manner before allowing the cup and saucer to fall from his grasp. His eyes widened momentarily in dreamy surprise as the room swirled about him, he slumped backwards unconscious in the chair.

'Sweet dreams,' said Sexton, smiling at last. 'Time to escort you to your new home.'

* * *

When Ralph Northcote regained consciousness, he found that he was lying on a camp bed in a darkened chamber, illuminated by one dim electric light bulb dangling above his head. As the clouds of the drug slowly dissolved and his vision and mind stumbled back into focus, gradually he was able to take stock of his new surroundings. He saw that he was in a vaulted cellar, the limed walls of which were grubby and blemished with patches of green mould at irregular intervals. Confused as to where he was and why he was here, he tried to drag his body into a sitting position but had great difficulty in doing so. In fact he failed. Something was preventing him. It took his hazy mind a few seconds to realise why. His left hand was handcuffed to the metal bed head.

He was a prisoner.

Again.

He could not move from the confines of the bed.

Panic and distress overwhelmed him in an instant and he screamed. His utterance was loud and inarticulate, like a wounded animal caught in a trap – which in essence he was. Strangely he found some comfort and solace in screaming, so he continued. With his eyes screwed tight and his fingers clenched, he bellowed at the top of his voice.

Suddenly a door at the end of the dank chamber opened and a figure in a white coat entered. Northcote ceased yelling and, opening his eyes, he stared at the figure in disbelief as it approached the bed.

It was Francis Sexton.

'Ah, you've returned to the land of the living, eh?' he said smoothly, moving towards the bed, a self-satisfied grin touching his shadowy features. 'Strong stuff that tea.'

Northcote shook his head in a desperate attempt to dislodge this hallucination from his sight. This mad vision. Was he dreaming? Was this really happening? Or was he going crazy?

'What… what the hell is going on?' he asked, his voice tired from all his screaming, now reduced to a hoarse whisper.

'Welcome to your new home.' Sexton threw his arms out

in a theatrical gesture to encompass the gloom.

Northcote shook his head miserably. 'I don't understand.'

'There's not a lot to understand. Simply, you're my prisoner now.'

'Prisoner? Why?' Northcote tugged on the handcuff. 'Why have you done this?'

'Because it suits my purposes, my plans.'

'What plans?'

'Oh, I don't think you need concern yourself with those for the moment. They do not require your active participation. Let us just say that you are simply my insurance, my alibi.'

Northcote felt a wave of despair crash over him. He didn't know what Sexton meant but he knew that he was in deep trouble. 'You can't do this to me,' he wailed. 'You and I were going to be partners…'

'Were we? In your dreams, my dear fellow. Why should I associate myself with an insane murderer?'

'You know I'm not insane.'

Sexton gave a little shrug as a wry smile touched his features briefly. 'Maybe I do, but that's not what the authorities think and will continue to think once I set to work.'

Northcote shook his head in confusion. The effects of the drug were still fogging his mind. 'What are you going to do?'

Sexton chuckled. 'Couldn't possibly tell you. Don't you know careless talk costs lives?' His laugh grew louder, echoing loudly inside Northcote's brain.

'Sweet dreams,' added Sexton softly as he made to leave. 'Don't let the bed bugs bite.' He switched out the light and closed the door. In the pitch darkness, Northcote could hear the key turning in the lock.

SIX

The vicarage of St Saviour's was a run down affair. The crumbling Victorian edifice had been an impressive adjunct to the church in its day but now it was in serious need of repair with damp and mould making a major invasion both inside and out. Father James Sanderson used only a few of the rooms, the rest were closed up and left for the insidious decay to take possession. It crossed my mind that it would almost be a blessing if the building received a direct hit on a Nazi bombing raid – providing no one was hurt – so that the place could be put out of its misery.

When I called that evening, Father Sanderson was just washing up a few dishes from his evening meal. He bade me take a seat by the meagre fire and offered me a cup of tea. Soon I would be awash with the stuff.

'I didn't expect to see you so soon,' he said, sitting opposite me. 'Don't tell me that you've made some progress already.'

'I won't tell you, because I haven't, but I realise that I need to know more about Annie Salter so I can start building up some theories. It's all a bit vague at the moment.'

This was a soft start to the questioning. I had decided to bide my time for the moment.

Sanderson shrugged his shoulders. 'I don't think I'm going to be much help to you. I doubt if I can tell you any more that I have already. I didn't know the woman's background all that well.'

'Who did?'

He shrugged again. 'I'm not sure.'

'What about neighbours?'

'Well, Annie was a very private person, she kept herself to herself but I believe she was quite friendly with the chap next door. Archie Dawson. He's an artist, cartoonist. He does a strip in one of the kids' comic cuts. He's at number 14. I got the impression from what she said that he kept a kindly eye on her.'

'Anyone else?'

'Not that I know of.'

'What about Annie's son?'

Sanderson screwed up his face as though he were in pain. 'He was a little devil. Got himself into trouble with the law before the war. I reckon if he hadn't gone into the army, he'd be back in gaol now.'

'Did he have any friends locally?'

'Malcolm made enemies not friends. You're not thinking that there's someone who might have a grudge against Malcolm who'd take it out on his mother?'

It was my turn to shrug. 'Not really. It would be a little convoluted and as the boy is dead there'd be little point. But, I suppose, stranger things have happened. I'm not ruling anything out yet.'

'You know best. You're the detective.'

These words did not cheer me. They just reminded me of the burden I was carrying. I remembered that earlier in the day I had regarded this case as a challenge. In a few short hours it had become a burden. Oh dear!

'What regiment was Malcolm assigned to?'

'The London Regiment, I think.'

'And there was no other member of the congregation that Annie was friendly with?'

Father Sanderson thought for a moment. 'Well, she shared the flower rota for the church with Mrs Dewhurst, Rita Dewhurst. I don't think the two women had much in common but they did sort of work together.'

Father Sanderson gave me her address and I made notes of all these names in my little notebook, although this procedure did not fill me with much hope. All they promised were a series of bland conversations à la Mrs Coulson. I reckoned it was time to grasp the nettle. If I was to get anywhere with this case, there was no room for holding back or pussy-footing around.

'Well,' I said, rising from my chair, 'thanks for your help, but no thanks for your hindrance.'

To my great satisfaction Sanderson's jaw dropped. 'I'm sorry,' he said, his voice full of uncertainty.

'And so am I. To be honest Father, I am puzzled. Do you really want me to find the murderer of Annie Salter?'

'Why bless you, of course I do.'

'Then I must ask you to stop prevaricating. You know more than you've told me. You have given me only half a tale and expect me to work with that. If Annie Salter was murdered, you know why. She has been distressed for some time. There was no one closer to her than you. She must have unburdened herself to you. But, for some reason, you and God were unable to help her. It was your guilt that led you to engage me, wasn't it?'

The priest turned from me, his body shaking with emotion. He muttered something but I did not catch what he said.

'Tell me,' I said, my voice rising in frustration. 'Help me.'

'I cannot,' he muttered, swinging around in the chair to face me once more, his eyes moist with tears.

'She told you something, didn't she? In confessional? That's what the box is for, after all, isn't it? For people to tell you their horrid truths. I reckon that she told you something that made you aware that she was in great danger. Greater than you realised.'

Father Sanderson said nothing but I could see from his

expression and the haunted look in his damp eyes that I was on the right track.

'So when you found her hanging there, murdered, you wrote a suicide note in a strange hand to help convince the police that it was murder. But, unfortunately for you, they weren't having any of it.'

'You are a clever detective, after all,' said Father Sanderson, allowing himself a slight smile. 'How do you know?'

'Because you are not such a clever deceiver.' I fished the suicide note out of my pocket. 'This paper was torn out of a notebook. It is the identical kind of notepaper, in fact, on which you wrote Mrs Frances Coulson's address for me.' With a flourish I now produced this sheet and matched the two together.

'Careless, but not conclusive,' I continued. 'However, although you tried to disguise your handwriting in the note, you could not quite eradicate some of your own stylistics. The squashed 'e' and the little flourish on top of the 'o', for example. There is much personality in an individual's handwriting and like certain facial features, they are difficult to disguise. To be fair, you did quite well, but not well enough. On top of all that there was a small red stain in the bottom left corner. Communion wine, I suspect'.

Father Sanderson ran a bony hand through his thick crop of grey hair. 'I can see that I seriously underestimated you, Johnny.'

'It's easily done. Usually with just cause – but not in this instant. Anyway, now it's time to come clean and tell me all. Why was Annie Salter murdered? What was her dangerous secret?

'I cannot tell you what she told me in the confessional. You know that. It is against the strict laws of my calling. It is between her and God.'

'So where do you fit into this relationship? As an errant eavesdropper? I am sure God would approve of you helping me catch a murderer.'

Father Sanderson shook his head and placed his hand on his heart. 'I would like to, my son, but I just cannot.'

With a great effort – and it was a great effort – I contained my anger for the moment. My instinct was to grab the old cleric and shake him violently until he spilled the beans, but what stopped me was my respect for a man of the church and, more particularly, the belief that even if I shook the fellow until his teeth fell out, he still wouldn't tell me.

'You are right,' he said slowly. 'I was the first to find Annie and I did write the note before I went round to see the police. I thought that if I convinced them that the note was written by someone else, they'd believe it was a murder and investigate. In this way I wasn't betraying any of Annie's confidences.'

'Isn't it a sin to let the murderer go free?'

'I don't know who the murderer is, Johnny. Please believe me. I just knew that Annie was fearful of something from her past.'

She had good reason to be, I thought. 'There are things you know that are vital to this case. You must help me.'

Sanderson simply shook his head gently in reply.

I don't know whether it was tiredness combined with a mixture of the remaining fragments of my own grief and blind frustration, but I exploded with anger. A fierce fury took hold of me, rippling through my body like an alien possession. All my previous restraint shot out of the window. I jumped up, grabbed hold of the cleric's shoulders and gripped them tightly, dragging him to his feet. 'Tell me,' I roared. 'Tell me what you know, you stupid old fool.' I bellowed the words as though I was reciting someone else's script. It wasn't me who had turned into this ranting bully: I had become another person who was inhabiting my skin. For a few fleeting moments Sanderson looked terrified and then a kind of strange serenity settled on his features. He offered no resistance to my violence and made no attempt to wrench himself from my grasp.

'I can't, Johnny,' he said, his voice a frail whisper. 'I can't.' His lips trembled with emotion. As he gazed at me with his sad and serene eyes, my anger subsided. It went as quickly as it had arrived. I could feel the heat and tension leaving my body. I felt weak and ashamed. With a sigh, I released Father Sanderson from my grip and he slumped back down in a chair, while I stood before him, disheartened and embarrassed.

Neither of us spoke for quite some time and then slowly Sanderson moved to a cupboard by the door and retrieved an item from within.

'There is something I can give you that may help.' In his hand he held a key. 'It is Annie's house key,' he said. 'She gave me a spare when she had that attack of influenza some years back. She was frightened that she might be trapped in the house too ill to move… Her house is empty now and will be for a few weeks. Maybe you could go there and investigate. There may be a clue, something to help...' His words trailed away and he held out the key to me.

'Maybe…' I said quietly. I took the key and left. There were no further words to say. Only I wish I had said them. I wish I had apologised for my threatening behaviour. But I didn't know that would be the last time I saw Father Sanderson alive.

SEVEN

Patience was a virtue. Francis Sexton knew that. It was one of those clichés that actually had a basis in truth. Indeed, he was well aware that it was not only a virtue, but in his case, it was essential. However tempted he was to begin his operations, he must not give way to such desires. Oh, yes, he longed to be out there in the darkness seeking victims, seeking to satiate his appetite for blood.

But he must wait.

He had waited this long. A few more nights would not hurt. His plan, carefully plotted and executed had taken months to reach fruition: to spoil it all now with rash and ill-prepared actions would be foolish and possibly ruinous.

Two more nights and then the feasting could begin.

EIGHT

The cleaner found Father Sanderson the next morning. His body lay sprawled on his back on the kitchen floor amidst a scattered array of broken crockery. His eyes were wide open, bulging from their sockets and his tongue lolled out of the side of his mouth.

He had been strangled.

The cleaner did not know this was the cause of death. It was the police pathologist who established this fact and informed Detective Inspector David Llewellyn who in turn informed me.

'Why are you telling me?' I asked casually as I lit a cigarette, just managing to conceal the shock I felt at learning that my client had been brutally murdered. I was immediately reminded of my unreasonable treatment of the old priest the previous evening. How I had shouted at him and shook him. An icy wave of remorse surged through my body, but I fought hard to retain my poise. I knew all too well that in situations like this guilt and regret were futile emotions.

It was round ten o'clock in the morning and I had been slow to get my act together that day. I'd had a restless night and then as dawn began to break, I slipped into a deep sleep, only surfacing well after my usual get-up time. I had only just shaved and breakfasted – a grand phrase for coffee and the stale doughnut I had snared creeping out of the larder cupboard – when my old copper buddy came a calling.

I knew this would not be a purely social call. It never was with David. Hence my question.

David raised an eyebrow in a whimsical fashion at my

query and smirked.

I smirked back. 'You don't usually call in and give me the low-down on your latest investigation – the new corpse in view – without an ulterior motive.'

'You know the victim.'

I nodded. 'Yes, he conducted Max's funeral. You were there. You saw him.'

'You know him better than that.'

I frowned. 'I'm sorry. Am I missing something?'

'Your name and telephone number were on a piece of paper found in the dead man's pocket.'

'So...'

'So, indeed. Tell me about it.'

I ran my fingers through my hair and sighed. I knew this was no time for subterfuge. 'I was doing a little job for him,' I admitted reluctantly.

David sat in a chair opposite me, his trilby nestling neatly in his lap. 'I think you're going to have to be a bit more explicit, boyo.'

'I was afraid of that.'

David grinned. 'A cup of tea is a fine accompaniment to a good yarn. You still got a kettle or do you suck the tea leaves through your teeth?' He chuckled at his own joke.

I brewed up a tarry cuppa for us both and told him my story.

'So,' said David slowly, when I had finished, drawing out the preposition to infinity, 'he was killed because he knew something. He was silenced. Whoever murdered him was worried that the old priest's conscience would override his religious convictions and that he would blab.'

I could not fault David's logic and I confirmed this with a nod.

'Any ideas?' he asked.

'At this moment, no.'

'But you will have?'

Possibly.'

'Probably – in fact knowing you, definitely.'

'You have more faith in me that I have.'

'I know you, Johnny Hawke. You are a terrier. Tenacious and impudent. You'll worry at this until something happens. You don't like to be beaten. Unfortunately, you also like to play the solitary game, but that is something you cannot do in this case. It may have started out as a private investigation, but now the Yard is involved it is a police matter with all the ramifications that phrase holds. Murder. Police matter. Understand, Johnny? Any information relevant to this investigation that you dig up or stumble over must be passed on to me.'

I saluted. 'Sir.'

'Yes, very funny. But I mean it. We're pals. Let's stay that way.'

'Of course,' I said, slipping my right hand out of view beneath my desk where I crossed my fingers. 'I'll share everything with you.'

David drained his mug of tea and slapping his trilby back on his head, sighed heavily in such a way that clearly indicated that he thought he was wasting his time with me.

'I'll be seeing you,' he said as made for the door.

'Of course, you will,' I grinned.

* * *

Within ten minutes of David's departure, I was leaving my office also. I had a house to search.

Annie Salter's terrace cottage was in a row up a narrow pathway at right angles to the main road. Her tiny garden which had obviously been tended with care was showing signs of neglect. The new growths of spring, bulbs and daffodils were in contention with weeds and hay grass. When entering a property illegally, one should always do so with confidence as though what you are doing is natural and official. Never skulk or look around nervously. Those are my rules, anyway.

As it happened on this bright March day, the coast was apparently clear: there wasn't a soul in sight.

Passing through the front door one was immediately in a small hallway and before you knew it, you found yourself in the parlour. It was tidy but cramped and smelt of damp. There was an ancient three piece suite, a mahogany sideboard bulky radio. A large mirror hung over the fireplace which caught my reflection and for a split second sent my blood racing because I thought I had company. I indulged in a quick rummage through the drawers of the sideboard but there didn't seem anything there of relevance to the case. Of course, I was searching blind. I really didn't know what I was looking for and as a consequence I had not an inkling what would be useful. I just hoped that something would jump out at me.

Annie had a secret, a secret that someone was prepared to kill for. Two people had died in order for the secret to remain. Would it be something obvious, if one knew where to look or would it be hidden – this mysterious something?

I moved into the kitchen. It was dark with only one small window by the sink to give illumination. There was a rough wooden table and two chairs. One still lay turned on its side. The one used in her hanging. I shuddered at the thought. How had he done it? (I assume it was a man). How had he persuaded Annie – or forced her up onto the chair and put the noose around her neck? Was the poor woman too terrified to resist or was she resigned to her fate? Seeing the scene of her demise brought the horror of the situation with great force. Surely there was some sign that there was another presence in the room, in the house? I examined every dusty surface, every drawer in the room but it seemed a fruitless task. And then I found something under the sink. An empty cigarette packet. Ten Capstan Full Strength. It may be nothing, but I seemed to remember that Father Sanderson saying that Annie neither drank nor smoked. And, besides, Capstan Full Strength was very much a man's fag.

I went up the stairs and found an even more exciting discovery. There were two small bedrooms and a bathroom. The main bedroom was a tidy affair with various religious artefacts adorning the walls, but the other room, a tiny cramped chamber, contained a zed bed which had recently been occupied. And by the side of it was a saucer that had been used as an ashtray containing several stubs of cigarettes – Capstan Full Strength. It seems that Annie had a lodger. Someone had stayed with her one night at least. Now who would that be? Well, whoever it was, he'd long gone. There were no clothes or other personal possessions. No suitcase and no other signs of his occupation. Or so I thought at first, but then I noticed something sticking out from under the mattress; a little flap of paper. Pulling the mattress back, I revealed a crumpled old newspaper: the *Evening Standard*. Three weeks old to be precise. It was folded over at the accommodation section and there was a portion torn off. This little discovery brought a smile to my weary face.

I returned to Annie's bedroom and gave that further scrutiny. There was nothing of any real significance but I discovered a photograph album at the back of the wardrobe which I decided to take with me for further study.

I reckoned my job here was done. I'd hardly made giant strides in the investigation but it was clear that things were not as cut and dried as the police had believed them to be. Annie had had a man staying in the house and he may have been responsible for her death and even if he wasn't, he must know something about it. And maybe, the *Evening Standard* may help me track this fellow down.

* * *

I was just locking the front door when a lanky fellow with a wild bush of grey hair came up the neighbouring garden path. He was dressed in a smart oatmeal coloured overcoat with a garish painted tie at his neck. He grinned at me and gave a friendly wave.

'Are you going to be my new neighbour?' he said in a breezy fashion. This I assumed was the artist Archie Dawson.

I shook my head. 'No. I've just been doing an inventory of Mrs Salter's effects.' The lie came easily and smoothly. I've had years of practice at the art of dissembling.

'Oh, yes, very sad business,' he said, his features darkening. 'Lovely woman.'

'You knew her well?'

'Not really. Just to pass the time of day with really, but she often did me little kindnesses, like looking after my cat when I had to go away and letting me borrow some milk or tea when I forgot to stock up. I'm awfully absent minded.' The smile returned. 'A very Christian soul.'

I nodded sympathetically and then I tested the waters. 'She had someone staying with her just before… just before she died…'

'Yes. A friend of her son's I gather. He died you know, her son.'

'What was this friend's name?'

'Frank, I think. He was only here a short time. He'd been gone a week before Annie met her sad end.'

'What did he look like? You're an artist, aren't you? Could you draw him?'

Archie Dawson pursed his lips and furrowed his brow. 'Well, I could I suppose. But why? What's your interest in him?'

Good question, chum, I thought.

'It's a legal matter concerning Annie's estate. We may need to talk to this fellow.'

Mr Dawson did not seem convinced. I could tell he was about to refuse.

'It would be a great help,' I said. 'I could pay you for your efforts.'

His eyes flickered brightly at this news. 'Oh, very well, but it will only be a sketch.'

'That's fine,' I grinned.

'You better come in then,' he said, producing his front door key

Half an hour later I was ten bob poorer, but in possession of a nicely detailed drawing of Annie Salter's mysterious lodger.

NINE

He looked down at the street through the grimy window. The outside world carried on in its mundane fashion while he watched on with envy. People passed by, muffled against the chill wind, the odd motorcar purred past and even stray dogs roamed freely. He groaned softly as though suffering from some grinding abdominal pain. But the agony was in his mind rather than a physical ache. He was going crazy cooped up in the attic room like a bloody prisoner. Part of him wished that Marshall would find him and the whole business was over. In essence, he was living on borrowed time as it was. He was dead really. To die again – properly this time – might be for the best. It couldn't be worse than hiding away indoors during the daylight hours, frightened of noises, shadows, men in black felt hats. This was no life.

He'd even thought about giving himself up to the authorities, but he knew that Marshall could still get to him, even in police custody. The devil had ways and means, contacts and favours and his tentacles were long and deadly. He knew Marshall would not rest until he was six feet under.

Perhaps if he got away from London. Into the country somewhere. He'd need money though, more than he had now. Instinctively his hand strayed to his wallet. He knew exactly how much money he had in there. Not much and the rent was already overdue. He'd have to do another flit. It had better be tonight.

Of course, he had plenty of money. But he didn't want to touch it. Not just yet. He was too frightened to. He reckoned as soon as he got his hands on it, Marshall would turn up like a bad smell.

He sighed heavily, left the window and dropped on his back onto the bed. The rusty springs groaned at the pressure he put them under. He didn't even have a fag to ease his nerves. What he wouldn't give for a drag on a Capstan Full Strength. He stared at the cracked ceiling, eyeing the brown damp stains in a mindless fashion, waiting for the darkness of night to arrive.

* * *

The door of Inspector David Llewellyn's office opened silently and the visitor, who had not knocked, entered. David glanced up from his paperwork, an irritated frown creasing his forehead. He hadn't wanted to be interrupted, especially by some ignoramus who hadn't the courtesy to knock before entering.

He was about to express these thoughts when he observed that his visitor was Deputy Commissioner Bradshaw.

'Sorry to interrupt, David,' he said with great charm, sitting in the chair opposite his desk.

'That's all right, sir,' said David, shuffling the papers on his desk in a nervous fashion. A visit from such a senior officer like Bradshaw was a rarity and more than a little daunting. It usually indicated that some form of telling off was imminent. Suddenly, David felt like a naughty schoolboy facing his headmaster.

'I won't keep you,' said Bradshaw, eyeing David's nervous hands twitching with the sheets of paper. He was well aware what effect his presence was having on the inspector. Such reactions came automatically with the post. He was used to it and often turned it to his benefit. But he liked Llewellyn and had no need or desire perturb him more than necessary.

'I have some disturbing news, I'm afraid,' he said, getting

to the point. 'Ralph Northcote. He's escaped.'

At the mention of the name, David Llewellyn's stomach churned. Ralph Northcote. Those two words brought back so many dark memories: the cellar, the blood, the poor mutilated girl and that mad face with the raw flesh dangling from its grinning mouth. The stuff of his nightmares.

He ran his fingers through his hair. 'How? I thought that place was supposed to be secure,' he found himself saying, while his mind refused to eliminate those dreadful images.

'He's been playing a long game, it seems. Over the last few months he's been visited by a psychiatrist who is writing a book on the criminal mind. A fellow called Sexton, Dr Francis Sexton. All seemed quite innocent enough but a few days ago, Northcote attacked this Sexton in his cell and slipped on his hat and coat as a disguise and managed to do a bunk.'

David shook his head in disbelief. 'What bloody incompetence,' he snapped.

Bradshaw nodded. 'I have to agree with you there. It's easy to understand how complacency takes root in these madhouses, but there is no excuse for such slackness. Anyway, it's no good crying over spilt milk. The devil is out and on the loose. Because of your close connection with the case, I thought you ought to know.'

Close connection? I should bloody well say so, thought David, bitterly. I was the one who trapped the bastard, brought him to justice and got him locked away for life. Except he isn't locked away now, so all my efforts have been in vain. And some poor girl will pay the price, sure as eggs is eggs – powdered or not. With a grimace, he allowed these thoughts to simmer but remain unspoken.

'Have we any notion where he went? Have his old haunts been checked?'

'Of course; checked and double checked. Nothing. For the moment it seems he has gone to ground – biding his time. But leopards do not change their spots, I'm afraid. I do not think it will be long before he will be on the hunt again.'

David nodded in agreement. 'We should have hung the bugger.'

'Spilt milk, Inspector.'

'Please, sir, do keep me informed. If he does kill again, I want to be in on the investigation. I must be.'

'Of course. Your previous experience with him would be invaluable. In the meantime, we keep searching and...'

'Holding our breath?'

Bradshaw gave David a bleak smile. 'Yes, I'm afraid so.'

The Deputy Commissioner rose from his chair and made for the door.

'Thank you, sir. I appreciate the visit,' said David.

Bradshaw gave the inspector a brief tight smile and left.

David slumped back in his chair and swore softly. Whatever wind had been in his sails, on this brisk spring day, had been removed. In his career, the case which he had been most proud of, the arrest that had given him the greatest satisfaction had just been screwed up and dumped in the rubbish bin. It was enough to make a copper throw in the towel. He wouldn't, of course. That wasn't his style. Like Johnny Hawke, he was a terrier and would worry at a problem until it was dealt with. But, nevertheless, the news had stabbed him through the heart and he was infused with a mood of desolation.

After a few moments, he turned his attention once more to the papers on his desk. The top sheets formed the statement of the cleaner who discovered the dead body of Father Sanderson at St Saviour's Church. This matter seemed small beer compared with the escape of the madman Northcote. 'Come on, boyo,' he muttered to himself, 'focus.' But his self-chiding was to no avail: his mind was filled with the vision of Ralph Northcote's horrible bloodstained face.

TEN

I read a lot as a youth, especially at the orphanage. Books were my escape from the unpleasant day-to-day reality. Indiscriminately, I gobbled them up: Dickens, Sapper, Conan Doyle, Rider Haggard, Trollope and Edgar Wallace. Other lives, other worlds, other adventures provided a welcome escape route from my dreary institutionalised life. I continued reading avidly until the outbreak of war when events seemed to rob me of my appetite for fiction. And losing an eye did not help. But in my late teens and early twenties I was a habitué of the Marylebone Library, snatching books off their shelves at least once a week. It felt strange, like a sentimental homecoming, to step back through the portals of this building again after a gap of three or four years.

It still smelt the same, that aroma of old damp books and polish assailed my nostrils as of old. I stood in the entrance lobby, breathed in deeply and let the nostalgia engage my senses and entrance me for a while. Briefly I allowed it to take my back to a time when the world was kinder and my life less damaged. With a sigh, I shook off my melancholy and made my way to the reference section. Low and behold, the little stout lady with the straw-coloured hair wrapped in a tight bun who used to serve me was still on duty behind the counter. She looked exactly the same, her large tortoiseshell glasses perched precariously on her nose and her brow puckered in a permanent state of concentration. I was tempted to greet her like an old friend with a cheery smile and a warm handshake, but I knew she wouldn't remember me. Nevertheless her presence behind the desk was somehow comforting and reassuring. In these dreadful changing times, there were some things that stayed the same.

'How can I help you?' she said, the voice was brisk and efficient but tinged with friendliness.

I pulled the copy of the *Evening Standard* from my pocket. 'Have you got this edition in your files?'

Pushing her spectacles up her nose, she examined the paper and then nodded. 'We should have. It's quite recent. Just a moment.' She disappeared through a frosted glass-fronted door which bore the word PRIVATE in green lettering. While I waited, I gazed around the room, at the desks, some which were occupied by static silhouettes pouring over various volumes and periodicals. They were like figures in a still life that was beginning to fade with age.

In less than five minutes, Miss Tight Bun returned bearing a large cardboard box which she placed on the counter between us.

'This contains the last six weeks' editions of the *Standard.* You'll have to search for it, but the one you require should be there,' she announced and allowed herself the briefest of smile.

I thanked her and took the box away to one of the desks, becoming another static figure in the landscape.

It did not take me long to find the issue of the *Standard* I was after and to hone in on the page I needed: the page that had been disfigured by Annie's mysterious lodger. I could see now that the missing portion from the Accommodation Available section contained details of a bed and breakfast establishment at Aldbridge Street off the Old Kent Road: 'Reasonable Rates. Discounts for ex-servicemen. Mrs Booth, Windsor House'.

Cheap lodgings, in other words.

I grinned. Rarely had the following up of a clue resulted

in such a perfect result. Perhaps I was a fairly good detective after all.

I made a note of the address and returned the box to Miss Tight Bun.

'Did you find what you were after?' she asked, stroking the box as though it was some beloved pet.

'I did. Thank you.'

This seemed to please her greatly. Reluctantly, I bid her farewell. A figure from my past, my more settled times. I suspected that I would never see her again. It was a sad parting.

* * *

The Old Kent Road runs parallel with the Thames on the borders of Bermondsey and Rotherhithe. I made my way on foot across Tower Bridge and down this dusty and shabby part of London. It was shabby before the bombing, but now the rubble and shattered structures added further distress to its features. Travelling east, I encountered Aldbridge Street running off to the right. It was a narrow thoroughfare of down at heel houses with small overgrown gardens. It was a ghost street: there wasn't a soul in sight, not even an errant child playing out in the gutter or a stray dog or cat loping around. The place was dead and now I was haunting it.

Windsor House was about halfway along. It stood out from the rest because the door was clean and was not caked in grime and the steps appeared to have been swept. I knocked heartily using the great black knocker in the shape of some unidentifiable animal. I could hear the results of my efforts booming inside the building. I had not long to wait before the door opened and I found myself facing a pretty woman, dressed in a fairaisle sweater and slacks. She wore a turban but wisps of hair escaped the tight wrapping giving the effect of an auburn halo. She was short, not much over five feet, but her stance and demeanour suggested she was a bright and lively soul. She greeted me with a smile.

'Hello. Can I help you?'

I raised my hat and returned the smile. It was the only polite thing to do.

'Miss...?' I saw the ring and remembered the 'Mrs' bit in the ad, but a spot of flattery never goes amiss.

'Mrs. Mrs Booth. Cora Booth. Are you after a room?'

'Actually I'm looking for someone and I believe he may be one of your guests.'

'Oh?' The smile had faded now and she looked at me warily. 'Why are you looking for this person? Are you from the police?'

This was a situation I found myself in many times: the 'who the hell are you?' query. I was never quite sure what was the best way to respond. Admitting that I was a private detective often caused suspicion or fear or resentment – or all three. On the other hand, if I made up some cock-and-bull story about being a relative or an insurance agent with good news to impart, I was often asked questions that I couldn't answer and my cover story would be blown apart. In this instance I didn't even know the name of the person I was looking for. Taking a chance, I avoided replying to the lady's question. Instead I pulled out the sketch Archie Dawson had drawn for me of Annie's mysterious lodger.

'It's this fellow,' I said.

There was no mistaking the sense of recognition that passed over the woman's features on seeing the drawing.

'Mr Bristow,' she said. It was an unguarded, automatic response.

I nodded. 'So he is staying here.'

Mrs Booth could hardly deny it, but she didn't admit to it either. 'What do you want with the gentleman?'

'It's a private matter concerning his poor brother,' I said

softly, adopting what I hoped was a mournful expression 'He passed away quite recently in rather sad circumstances'.

'I see.'

'It was all rather upsetting. I wanted to pass on the news to him quietly.' I was virtually mouthing the words now in a soft unctuous whisper. They seemed to have their desired effect. Mrs Booth nodded sympathetically.

'Well, yes, Mr Bristow is one of my paying guests. How awful for him.'

'Yes,' I agreed. 'Is he at home now?'

'I believe he is. He rarely goes out during the day.'

'Well if I might see him, I can pass on the sad tidings and give him some comfort.'

'Yes, yes, of course.'

My performance had completely won over Mrs Booth who seemed as upset at the bereavement of Mr Bristow's phantom brother as though he were her own.

'Come in, Mr...?'

'Hawke. John Hawke.' I saw no reason to give a false name.

'He's on the top floor.'

It was a very tidy house which smelt of polish and disinfectant. Mrs Booth led me up three flights of stairs to the top of the building.

'This is Mr Bristow's room,' she announced in hushed tones and then tapped gently on the door. 'Mr Bristow,' she called. 'Mr Bristow, you have a visitor.'

There was no response. Mrs Booth threw me a puzzled glance. 'I felt sure he was in. I certainly haven't seen him go out today.

She knocked again – louder this time. Still there was no answer.

'Do you think he'll be all right?' I said. 'Perhaps he's ill?'

'Mr Bristow,' she called loudly, 'It's about your brother.'

Silence.

I stepped forward and tried the door. It was locked. This action did not please Mrs Booth.

'Mr Hawke,' she snapped. 'I'll remind you that this is my establishment. I can't have you rattling my guest's doors carte blanche.'

I looked suitably chastised. 'I'm sorry. Do you have a key? I mean the poor man may be laid out in there, too ill to respond.'

I could see that Mrs Booth considered my idea as arrant nonsense, but none the less she pulled out a bunch of keys from her trouser pocket and applied one to the lock of Bristow's room. She turned the handle and opened the door a few inches and called out her lodger's name once again. And once again there was silence.

Gingerly, she entered the room and I followed directly behind her.

The room was occupied.

A man stood by the far wall in the shadows. I couldn't see his face properly, but I did observe that he was holding a gun.

'Oh, Mr Bristow,' said Mrs Booth, seeing the shadowy figure and then added, 'Oh, Mr Bristow,' an octave higher when she saw the gun.

'Get away from the door,' he snapped, taking a step forward.

We did as he asked.

'You're not going to use that, are you, Mr Bristow?' asked Mrs Booth.

'As long as you don't interfere with me. Now get right over there. I'm leaving.' So saying he moved swiftly towards the door. I wasn't about to let this fellow slip though my grasp so easily, gun or no gun. I stuck my leg out and he stumbled. I was on him in an instant. I jumped on his back and had my arms around his neck as he staggered forward, carrying me piggy-back style on to the landing.

With a gruff cry, he reversed with great force, ramming me against the wall, smashing my right elbow into the plaster. An electric shock of pain ran up my arm and I released my grip sufficiently for Bristow to pull away.

He now swung round and beat me on the head with the gun. Luckily, I had kept my hat on which softened the blow a little, but nevertheless I did see stars and my legs wobbled and gave way. With a grim reluctance I slumped down to the floor.

He swung back his leg with the intention of booting me in the face, but I managed to grab hold of the speeding limb as it approached me and yanked it upwards, causing his owner to lose his balance. With a yell of surprise, Bristow flew backwards, towards the edge of the staircase where he tottered briefly at the top of the landing before crashing down the flight of stairs to the floor below.

I pulled myself to my feet and peered over the banister. Bristow looked dazed and dishevelled, but was already pulling himself to his feet. On seeing me gaze down upon him, he aimed the pistol in my direction and fired two shots. I dodged down and heard the fierce missiles whiz past me and lodge in the plaster behind me. At this point, Mrs Booth, who had been strangely silent through the shenanigans, began to whimper and shake.

Bristow let off two more shots, keeping me well away from the top of the stairs and then there was silence apart from the bleatings emanating from the distressed landlady.

At length, I peered down to the floor below but, as I suspected, there was no sign of my quarry. He had bolted. I ran down the stairs, along the hallway and out into the street, but there was no sign of Bristow in either direction. He had carried out a very effective disappearing act.

* * *

Twenty minutes later I was sitting in Mrs Booth's parlour, administering a large glass of brandy to the shaken lady. She had stopped whimpering and the tears had ceased, but she still shivered as though she were sitting on a block of ice.

'You are from the police, aren't you?' were the first coherent words she spoke since entering the room.

'Not quite,' I said, lighting a cigarette in an attempt to calm my nerves. Despite my occupation, I wasn't used to being shot at in the afternoon in a respectable boarding house.

'What does 'not quite' mean?'

'I am a private detective.'

'Why didn't you tell me? Why didn't you warn me?'

'To be honest, I didn't realise there was anything to warn you about. I didn't realise this chap would be violent – that he had a gun.'

'Who is he?'

I shrugged my shoulders. 'I don't know. Yet. He's involved in a mysterious death I'm investigating, but at the moment I don't know how he's involved.'

'Well, he was certainly determined you weren't going to catch up with him.'

I nodded. 'I reckon he was more frightened than aggressive. He didn't use his gun until the last moment.'

Mrs Booth gave me one of her whimpers. 'But he did use it. In my house. My respectable house.' The tears began again and I placed my hand on her shoulder in a feeble attempt to comfort her. I felt guilty at having put the poor creature through this ordeal, for having placed her in danger. I never thought my visit would turn out in such a dramatic fashion, but perhaps I should have considered the possibility.

'Shouldn't we call the police?'

'I don't think that would be wise. It might get your place a bad reputation: harbouring gunmen and such...'

Her look told me she needed little persuading in this matter.

'You don't think he'll come back, do you?'

I gave her a grim smile. 'That's the last thing he will do. He's off to pastures new – wherever they may be.'

This seemed to reassure her and she took another swig of brandy. 'And he owed me back rent,' she said softly as though she was speaking to herself.

So my friend Bristow – if that was his real name, which I doubted – was short of the readies.

'If you don't mind, I'd like to pop back up to his room and have a look around. See if I can find any clues as to where he'll go next.'

'I suppose so. It'll be a while before I have the courage to go back up there myself.' She reached over and poured herself another measure of brandy.

* * *

It was a bleak room. Being the attic, the outer wall sloped down almost to the floor with a dormer window fixed at its centre, through which the occupant had a fine view of the street below. I noticed an ashtray by the bed containing a stack of tab ends – Capstan Full Strength. Apart from these scorched souvenirs, the mysterious lodger, Mr Bristow, had left behind very few possessions, most of which were scrunched up in a small brown case: underwear, a few shirts, socks and similar items. There was however a small envelope secreted in the lid containing a couple of photographs. One was of Mr Bristow himself in army uniform with another chap, tall, saturnine and decidedly shifty. The other was a studio shot of a lady I recognised. It was Annie Salter. Glancing on the back of the snapshot of Bristow, I saw in neat pencil the words Private Malcolm Salter and Lance Corporal Marshall. Looking at the pictures again I could see the similarity of features shared by Bristow and Annie. For it was clear that Bristow was indeed Annie's son. And lo and behold, he was alive and kicking, returned from the dead. That was part of Annie's terrible secret. Her ne'er-do-well son had not been killed at Dunkirk. Now he was on the run, but there was something about his behaviour that told me that he was terribly frightened of someone or something. Involuntarily, I shivered, as I realised that I was wading into deeper and darker waters.

ELEVEN

He tingled with a strange mixture of excitement and confidence. It had been a long process and now he was about to realise his ambition. He had waited in the wings for so long and now he was about to step out into the spotlight – a very dark spotlight. It was his due. He had endured months of waiting patiently while he built up his relationship with Ralph Northcote, cultivating the man's intimate friendship, slowly and gently persuading him that there was a fully active killing-and-eating life waiting for him outside the drab walls of his prison. 'Drab walls of his prison' – this last phrase made him smile. Northcote had a far worse prison now, enduring a mere existence rather than a life. But that was his own fault: he hadn't been clever or perceptive enough to be suspicious of the all too accommodating Sexton. Greed and self interest alone had governed his actions and blinded him from the truth.

Well, thought Sexton with a sardonic grin, tonight I am going to enhance your bloody and notorious reputation. Tonight I will kill and feast in your name. He waited in the shadows, in a shop doorway near the municipal hall. It was late but he could still hear the strains of the small band playing inside. A jolly dance to cheer up the tired and jaded natives of old war-ravaged London Town. Sexton imagined the scene inside. A group of geriatric musicians in tired and shiny dinner suits on stage churning out a series of old tunes in three-quarter time, the room misted with cigarette smoke and a motley crew of dancers shuffling around the floor, trying desperately to forget the war, the blackout, the bombing, the deaths and their deprived miserable lives. There would be a few servicemen on leave on the hunt for a goodnight kiss and a fumble afterwards; a few grannies and grandads showing off, dancing with annoying panache; and guilty wives having a quick waltz with a stranger while their hubby was away fighting for King and country overseas. Sexton smoked several cigarettes while he waited, waited patiently, enjoying the taste of the tobacco as it mingled with the cold night air. Eventually the music stopped and the dancers began to leave, stepping out into the dark spring night, their voices bright and chatty, carrying some of the pleasure of the evening with them.

A group of four girls bustled by him, giggling and humming one of the dance tunes. Individually, each was ideal for his purposes, but bunched together as they were there was no chance to select just one of them. Others left the hall in dribs and drabs. A couple seemed to be having an argument on the hall steps. He was a loutish youth with greasy hair, wearing a pin-striped suit that was too big for him. She was a plump girl with an explosion of frizzy blonde hair and a stupid face. He was pulling her arm, trying to persuade her to go one way, while she was of a mind to go in the other. Sexton couldn't hear what they were saying, but the boy was particularly angry, his voice lowered to a vicious staccato rasp. She started to cry and with a snarl he pushed her away from him and turned to go. Now she seemed undecided and took a step in his direction but he had walked off at such speed that he had disappeared into the night.

For a moment, the girl stood unsure what to do, apart from stifle her sobs with a handkerchief. And then with a dejected sigh, she set off in the opposite direction from the boy, moving along the pavement towards where Sexton was hiding. His pulse quickened. She could be the one if he was lucky. He had picked the spot carefully. Two hundred yards further down the road there was a small park where he had planned to could carry out his work undisturbed.

The street was now empty and quiet apart from the click clack of the girl's heels on the damp pavement. When she had passed by him, Sexton untangled himself from the shadows and began following her at a discreet distance. Caught up with her own emotions the girl had no sense of the dark shape that was slowly but inexorably bearing down on her.

'Excuse me, Miss,' he called softly as they reached the open park area.

Instinctively, the girl turned around to observe the silhouette of a tall man carrying a suitcase.

'Excuse me,' he said again, as he stepped forward, close to her, so close that she could see his face in the moonlight which filtered through the straggly night clouds. It was pale and strained and the eyes looming behind large spectacles were strange and somehow hypnotic.

'I wonder if you can help me,' he said, placing his suitcase at his feet.

The girl did not know how to respond to his request. She just stared at the stranger blankly. He gave her an odd smile and then, before she knew what was happening, he had his gloved hands around her throat. It happened so swiftly that she hadn't time to cry out. Her eyes widened in terror and her body rippled in panic, briefly as she began to struggle, but his grip on her throat was too strong and she quickly lost consciousness, slumping like a large rag doll against her assailant.

Quickly he dragged her into the bushes and found a space big enough to lay her down. He then retrieved his suitcase. In the cover of the bushes he began to undress the girl. Slowly and methodically he removed all her clothing in order to reveal her naked form. Taking off his gloves, he ran his fingers over her skin, his head buzzing with excitement, his sexual juices flowing. Then he slipped off his overcoat and placed it neatly on the ground some distance away from the body. Underneath he was wearing a protective white smock. With nervous fingers he opened the suitcase, withdrew the instruments and with precise deliberation began the butchering process.

Some fifteen minutes later, the smock now spattered liberally with blood, he had removed the organs and limbs he required and wrapped them in muslin and newspaper which he carefully stowed away with the instruments in the case. He gazed down with satisfaction at the girl's mutilated body which glistened in the pale light. He dipped his fingers in one of her wounds and then sucked them dry. A little appetiser before the feast that would follow.

As some far away clock chimed the midnight hour, he stepped from the bushes with his suitcase and its grisly contents and with calm deliberation headed for home.

TWELVE

I spent the night at the cinema with Peter. I had befriended this runaway orphan in the early part of the war* and through various incidents and adventures, I seemed to have become his unofficial guardian. He was now looked after by two spinster sisters, Edith and Martha Horner, but I kept a fatherly eye upon him and tried to provide him with the care and guidance I'd lacked as a child. However, I had neglected my duty somewhat in recent weeks, indulging in my grief over the loss of Max. But now I was determined to make amends.

I picked him up early for the Horner's neat little villa and treated him to fish and chips – a slap up meal, he called it – followed by the best seats at the Odeon, Leicester Square. I knew that apart from my neglect, the lad needed cheering up. His first big romance had crashed into the buffers and the experience had hit him hard. Poor sod. Although he had no biological connection with me, he seemed to have inherited by some weird kind of osmosis a very tender shell where affairs of the heart were concerned. Well, the greasy fish and chips followed by Abbott and Costello's antics as they 'Hit the Ice' along with a tub of ice cream cheered him up considerably and he was a lot chirpier on the way out of the cinema than he had been on his way in.

We found a little café open in Beak Street, and concluded the evening with a cup of tea. As usual Peter was eager to hear about my latest case, but I directed the conversation away from this particular topic. If his romance had hit the buffers, so, it seemed, had my investigations into Annie

* *see the first Johnny One Eye novel,* ***Forests of the Night***

Salter's death. It had been a revelation to discover that her son was still alive and had been dossing down with her for a while and that now it seemed he was in hiding. Well, he was officially dead, so the authorities would not take too kindly to him still breathing the civilian air of London when he should be in the army. Circumstances suggested that he may well have killed his mother, but something told me otherwise. I'm no Sherlock Holmes: this wasn't a deduction – just an instinct. But carrying a shooter – and, indeed using it – clearly indicated that Master Salter was a bit of a villain. A nice fact to establish, but unfortunately the blighter had slipped through my fingers and was somewhere out there in this vast city impersonating a needle in a hay stack. The sudden recollection of this sad fact must have found its way onto my features.

'What's up? You look miserable,' Peter observed, gazing at me over the lip of his mug of tea.

I shrugged. 'Nothing important,' I replied, glancing at my watch. 'Hey, it's time I was taking you home. It's school tomorrow.'

Peter frowned. 'Hey, don't treat me like a kid. I'm fourteen you know and mature with it.'

I grinned. 'I'm not. I've got a little problem with trying to find someone. It's niggling me. That's all.'

'Tell me about it. I might be able to help. Remember, when I'm fully grown up, I'm going into the detective business too.'

I was about to say, 'over my dead body', but thought better of it. I didn't want to tempt fate. 'O.K. And then we get you in a taxi and home.'

Peter nodded with enthusiasm.

I gave him an abbreviated version of events while over dramatising the tussle I'd had with Malcolm Salter alias Mr Bristow on the top floor of Windsor House in order to disguise my incompetence at allowing him to escape.

Peter listened eagerly and narrowed his eyes in a sage-like fashion when I had finished. 'So,' he said, 'your problem now is to find out where this Bristow/Salter character has gone to ground.'

'That's one of them.'

'What does he look like?'

I reached inside my pocket for the sketch but changed my mind. Instead, I slipped out the photograph of Malcolm Salter I'd taken from his room in Windsor House. 'That's the chappie,' I said. 'Innocent looking cove, isn't he?'

Peter's eyes widened. 'Who is the other man?'

I shook my head. 'A mate of his from the army, I suppose. The name on the back of the snap says he's Lance Corporal Marshall – no first name.'

'I've seen that face before. I am sure of it.'

'Really? Are you sure?'

Peter nodded emphatically. 'Yes,' he said, drawing the word out as he narrowed his eyes. 'Of course… He's in my scrapbook.'

'Your scrapbook?'

'Yes, my crime scrapbook.'

'Explain, young master.'

'I keep a scrapbook of newspaper cuttings connected with big crimes. I follow the progress of their investigation – or lack of it – and make notes. It's good training for when I start as a detective.'

'I'm sure it is,' I said without much conviction. 'So who is this chap,' I pointed at the Lance Corporal.

'I think he was mixed up with an armed robbery in Chelmsford a couple of months ago. Can't really remember properly – but it's in my files.'

'In your scrapbook.'

Peter's eyes flashed brightly and nodded. 'Yes.'

'I think you'd better let me have a look at this scrapbook of yours.'

* * *

Later that night, I sat in my office, a small glass of Johnnie Walker in my mitt and Peter's scrapbook on my desk. I was reading an account of an armed robbery at the Benson Road branch of the Midland Bank in Chelmsford. Two men had entered the small branch just as it was about to close one Wednesday in late February. Once inside, they shut the doors and revealed they were carrying weapons. One had a shotgun, the other a pistol – recognised as an army pistol by the only teller on duty, a Mr Percy Crabtree. Both men wore handkerchiefs across the lower part of their faces to hide their features. The robber who appeared to be the leader – the one that did most of the talking – wore a dark blue felt fedora. There were only three customers in the bank at the time and these were made to stand facing the wall by the thief with the pistol while the other forced the teller to open the safe. Being Wednesday the safe contained the cash for wages of two local factories and the thieves managed to bag over two thousand pounds.

As they were leaving, one of the customers made a grab for the robber. He was a young lad who was just about to join the army and had a fit of the heroics. He managed to knock Mr Fedora down and snatch the handkerchief from his face. In panic, the other robber shot him, wounding him badly in the thigh. Following this dramatic incident, both men fled with their haul.

The newspaper account was accompanied by an artist's impression of the unmasked felon. It was to my way of thinking, as it had been young Peter's, that the villain was none other than Lance Corporal Marshall. Blimey, I thought, the power of the artist's pencil had certainly been working in my favour today. So Lance Corporal Marshall was a nasty piece of work and no doubt his accomplice was Mr Bristow alias Malcolm Salter. So that's why he was hiding out. But where was Marshall and where was the loot? Salter certainly hadn't got it. He certainly hadn't been painting the town. Mrs Booth assured me he was hard up, owing her rent.

Well, in some ways the situation was a little clearer now but the solution was still as far away as ever. With this dismal thought, I headed for bed.

THIRTEEN

'She was discovered by an ARP Warden on his way home. He usually takes a short cut across the park and found the body lying on the pathway. Apparently she had been killed in the bushes…'

'But the murderer dragged the body out here so that she'd be discovered very soon,' said David Llewellyn finishing the uniformed sergeant's sentence for him. He'd been called out of bed early that morning by a telephone call from Deputy Commissioner Bradshaw. 'It looks like our friend has started his work again, Llewellyn. I reckon you'd better take charge of the business from the start. Get yourself down there pronto.'

And pronto, with the aid of a police driver, he had got himself down to Camden and the little park where the poor girl, Doreen Maberley, had been found.

'I still don't understand why he dumped the body out here where anyone could find her?' the sergeant was musing.

'To show off his handiwork, I suppose.'

'Handiwork is right. Poor girl: it looks like Jack the Ripper got at her. All her insides have been interfered with,' said the sergeant, having great difficulty in keeping his breakfast down.

'You've searched the area, I presume.'

'With a fine tooth comb, sir. I got two of my lads on it as soon as it was light. They've been over the ground half a dozen times. Nothing. Not even any shoe imprints. He's left the murder scene as clean as a whistle.'

Llewellyn knelt down by the corpse and examined it closely. 'He's taken the heart, liver and cut out her tongue.'

'What sort of man would do such a thing? He must be raving mad.'

'Mad, certainly. But not raving. He has a cunning intelligence with nerves of steel.'

'Blimey, sounds as though you know the blighter'.

Llewellyn sighed but said nothing.

Leaving the body in the capable hands of the pathologist from the Yard, the inspector departed the scene, taking in lungfuls of fresh air as he left the park. He couldn't remember feeling as depressed as he did now. The bastard he'd nailed all those years ago, the bastard he hoped would feel the hangman's noose around his neck, was free and had killed again. Killed? Well, it wasn't quite as simple as that. He had ripped and torn the flesh of a young girl to satisfy his appetite for flesh and blood. This wasn't just murder, it was mutilation and, God forbid, cannibalism. He shuddered at the thought of it.

And now his task was to find him, and find him fast before he was able to carry out another of his gruesome crimes. How on earth was he going to do that? He paused and lit a cigarette before climbing into the police car.

'Where to, sir?' enquired the driver, revving the engine. 'To the Yard, is it?'

'No,' said Llewellyn wearily. 'Priors Court, off the Tottenham Court Road.'

* * *

He felt good. He had hunted, killed and now he had dined on his spoils. He washed down the last of his bloody titbits with a glass of water – nothing stronger than water so as not to interfere with the taste – and sat back with a sigh of great satisfaction. He wiped his mouth and grinned. The whole experience had been as wonderful as he had anticipated. All that was left was to read an account in the press of his glorious escapade. Maybe in the evening edition. Certainly in the next day's nationals.

He lit a cigarette and puffed contentedly. It would be good to show the newspaper reports to Northcote: another twist of the knife, aggravating the wound. Idly, he thought of his prisoner as he blew smoke rings on the air. There he was in that dark chamber below, lying on his rank bed unable to do anything but sleep and regret. In the few days he had been incarcerated in the cellar, he had regressed into a child-like moronic state. Sexton was convinced this was the result of the shock he had suffered by having his dream of freedom so brutally snatched away from him and being tethered like an animal in a dank cell. Well, in reality, Northcote had fulfilled his usefulness. There was no real point in keeping the beast alive for much longer. He would only become a nuisance, like an ill pet one had to attend to on a daily basis.

As soon as Sexton was able to have the final pleasure of showing Northcote the newspaper story about the girl he'd killed and boast how tasty she had been, as soon as he was able to witness the wild rash emotions that this would raise within his captive, he would have done with the fellow.

And then he would snack off him.

FOURTEEN

It was just before noon when I arrived back at my office following my morning labours and found a note pushed under my door. It was from David Llewellyn. It read: 'Would really appreciate a chat. Can you make The guardsman at one o'clock? DL'

The Guardsman was a pub not far from Scotland Yard where David and I often met up to sup a few pints and moan about our respective investigations. I was intrigued and indeed thirsty, so I did a quick about face and headed off in the direction of that particular watering hole.

As I pounded the dusty streets of the capital, I thought over what I had learned that morning. I had taken myself down to the War Office and made contact with an ex-client of mine, Bobby Driscol, a good-looking lad with a club foot who had been wrongly accused of being involved in a dog doping scam at White City greyhound track a few years back. I had managed to prove his innocence and as a result he's been grateful ever since and always eager to do me a favour. He was only too happy to dig out some details for me concerning Private Malcolm Salter and his oppo Lance Corporal Marshall. In a sense, most of what I learned only confirmed what I had surmised, but it was reassuring to know I was on the right track. The two men had served with the London Regiment – but had not served for too long. The two had gone AWOL shortly after enlisting. They had joined that invisible platoon of deserters that somehow had blended back into civilian life without a trace. It always puzzled me how these men could manage to do that so effortlessly and, indeed, without conscience. They were selfishly turning their back on their country and its plight when they were needed most. I was sure that in the main it wasn't just a matter of cowardice; these blighters wanted to be free of the regimented restraints that the life in the forces brought.

Anyway, we now knew for certain that Annie's son did not die in battle. This was a lie; this was her secret, which she no doubt manufactured for respectability's sake. It would hurt her too much to admit that her son was a deserter. And, it would seem that the prodigal had returned home and was kipping down in her spare room. I was convinced that this secret was tied up with her murder. However, I found it hard to contemplate that her son was responsible for her death, but I couldn't discount it completely for I had encountered stranger and crueller things in my career.

I had never known The Guardsman be less than buzzing with business at lunchtime and today was no exception. As I opened the door to the saloon bar, I was met with a barrage of noise and raucous conversation from the crowd within: office workers snatching a quick dinner break, old folk whiling away their time, waiting for the war to end, soldiers, sailors and airmen on leave, along with some uniformed Yanks and various shady looking types, all enveloped in a fine mist of cigarette smoke and a web of chatter. And one other: a burly blonde-haired Welsh police inspector hunched on his usual stool at the end of the bar.

I was early for our one o'clock appointment, so he must have been much earlier. His stiff posture and sour expression indicated that he was not a happy man. Squeezing my way through the throng, I slipped onto the stool beside him and gave him a cheery grin.

'At last,' he said grumpily.

'I'm early.'

'Two more pints, Arthur,' he called the barman, who was

in the middle of serving two plump ladies. Arthur nodded.' Wait yer turn,' he called with a grin.

'So,' I said, 'you wanted to see me. I can tell by your expression it's not to tell me you've come up on the pools.'

'Too bloody true. It's bloody Ralph Northcote.'

The name rang a tiny bell in my memory, but not loud enough to bring the fellow to mind. My expression obviously conveyed my lack of comprehension.

'It was my first big case back in '35. He'd been killing girls, this Northcote. Killing them and then eating their flesh.'

I shuddered. Now the bell rang louder. I remembered the case. It was before I'd joined the force, before I'd lost an eye and before I knew David, but it was very big in the papers.

'What about him –this Northcote?'

'He's escaped and murdered again.'

'Crikey. Escaped?'

'From the nut house.' David ruffled his hair in frustration. 'The bastard should have been strung up and then this wouldn't have happened. All that work I did to get his conviction and then the bloody powers that be deemed he wasn't of sound mind. Course he wasn't of sound mind: he was a bloody murderer who ate his victims.'

The pints arrived and I paid for them. 'Have a gulp of this and try to calm down.'

David did as he was told. He devoured half the glass almost in one go. 'I had to talk to someone about it and I knew you'd understand more than any other,' he said, at length, wiping the froth away from his upper lip with the back of his hand.

'I'm flattered.'

David gave me a weary smile.

'Go on,' I said, 'give me the whole sad story.'

And he did – from Northcote's capture, arrest and

conviction up to that very morning when he'd been examining the mutilated body of a young girl who had been savaged in exactly the same way as Northcote's other victims.

'It's his work all right. The devil's resumed where he left off.'

'Was the girl's handbag or purse missing?' I asked.

David shook his head, 'Untouched.'

'So he must be OK for money. Where's he getting it from? Someone must be hiding him. Providing him with cash, food and shelter.'

David curled his lip unpleasantly. 'He caters for himself where food is concerned. But you have a point.'

'Were there any other associates from his past who are likely to sympathise with him – even share his predilections…?'

'Not that I know of. He was a lone wolf.'

'Mmm. I see a brick wall looming ahead.'

'So do I. Why do you think I'm in here drowning my sorrows?'

'It seems to me your best bet is to have a long in-depth conversation with this Dr Sexton chap. If he's been visiting Northcote on a regular basis, surely he would have learned something that would help. Some indication, some clue as to where he is and what his plans are.'

'I reckon I can guess what his plans are: to kill again and have a fleshy banquet. But, you are right. Sexton seems to be my only hope for the moment.'

'And where there is hope, there is a chink of light.'

David gave me a tight grin. 'I knew chatting to you would be good for me. Just telling you about it and expressing my frustration helps. It's a bit like a confessional.'

'Bless you, my son.'

David laughed briefly and then he added seriously, 'I

don't think my colleagues would fully understand what this Northcote business meant to me.'

I understood. In this respect David and I were alike. Rightly or wrongly, we became personally involved in our cases and cared greatly that we achieved justice and closure. David thought he'd had both with the Northcote affair but that particular rug had been well and truly dragged out from under him.

David ordered another round. I settled for a half this time. I wasn't in the mood for boozing. Alcohol sometimes helped me not only to relax, but also enabled my brain to see possibilities and scenarios concerning my investigations that the sober mind couldn't – but somehow today I just didn't fancy it. I wanted to keep a clear head.

'So, how are you getting on with your little murders: the Annie Salter and Father Sanderson business,' said David, looking and sounding more relaxed now that he'd unburdened himself to me and downed a couple of pints. 'I'm off the case now; the Northcote business has taken priority. So come on, spill the beans.'

Now it was my turn in the confessional. I told him all I knew so far. I saw no reason not to. I wasn't going very far with things at the moment. Maybe he could throw me a morsel of hope too.

When I had finished, my companion gave me a gloomy nod. 'Difficult,' he said slowly. 'That Chelmsford bank job. I know a bit about that. Old Percy Herbert's been assigned to the case. We know who the leader of the gang is.'

'Well it's Lance Corporal Marshall.'

'Yeah, but that's not his real name. Some of the boys at the Yard recognised him from that artist's impression in the paper. It's Bruce Horsefield. He did time before the war.'

I dragged out the photograph from my wallet with Salter and his mate. 'Is this him?' I asked.

'That's the boy. He worked himself up from street mugging to robbing a jeweller's shop in '36. Got four years for that. Then he disappeared. Obviously he changed his name but not the colour of his spots. I reckon he's a real wrong 'un.'

'And is Inspector Herbert anywhere near catching him?'

David grinned. 'Is he heck. Old Herbert has trouble catching a cold. I reckon Horsefield could run rings around him.'

'I suppose he's tried Horsefield's old haunts.'

'I suppose so. I don't really know. I only pick up bits of info in the canteen but I do know that Percy ain't making any progress.'

'Somehow that does not cheer me.'

David chewed his lip. 'I suppose I could let you have a copy of Horsefield's file. You might see something in there that Percy hasn't.'

'It might help.'

'I shouldn't, of course. It's strictly against the rules, you understand.'

'I understand.'

He gave me a quick wink 'I'll get a copy to you by tonight.'

No more was said on the matter and we sat for a while in silence, two weary detectives with unpleasant loads on our shoulders, deep in our separate tunnels with no light flickering at the end. Just darkness.

'Well,' David said at length, draining his glass, 'I either have another and fall down sozzled or get back to the office and bang my head against the wall.' He slipped off his stool. 'See you soon, Johnny boy. Good hunting.' With a brief smile he turned and squeezed his way towards the door.

I lingered over the dregs of my drink for some time

mulling over the case in general and what I had learned in particular. I sketched out in my mind a rough plan of action – a very rough plan – and then I too headed for the exit and some fresh air.

I spent the afternoon visiting another client: a simple marital job that I knew I could clear up within a week. I hated these jobs but they were my main means of earning a living – exposing some poor sod's infidelity.

As it was growing dusk, I found myself in Benny's café with a mug of tea and a salt beef sandwich. We chatted for a while in a desultory fashion, but I could see the old boy was tired, so I left him to lock up and made my way home. The lunchtime beer was still sloshing unpleasantly about in my stomach and I had no desire for more.

Arriving back at Hawke Towers, I found a brown envelope on the mat. David had been as good as his word – not that I doubted he wouldn't be. Inside the envelope were the file notes on Bruce Horsefield aka Lance Corporal Marshall. Here then was my bedtime reading.

FIFTEEN

Mrs Frances Coulson had only just bid one of her gentleman callers adieu and was enjoying a cigarette and a small glass of sherry, when her mellifluous doorbell rang. A frown manifested itself on her carefully made up face. She wasn't expecting anyone – she had no more appointments that day – and so this could only be some sort of inconvenience. As she made her way to the front door, she hoped it wasn't that detective fellow with the eye patch. He was too inquisitive and too sharp for comfort.

She could see a bulky shadow through the frosted glass. So it was a man.

With some trepidation she opened the door and on seeing her visitor, her mouth dropped open.

'Hello Auntie,' said the man. 'Aren't you going to invite me in?'

SIXTEEN

'So what do we know about this Sexton bloke, sir?' Sergeant Sunderland eased the car into third gear as he posed this query.

'Not a lot,' said David Llewellyn, glumly. 'He used to be a GP but now practises as some sort of psychiatrist. I suppose there's more money in doling pills out to the nervous and depressed. And he is supposed to be writing a book about the criminal mind.'

'I could give him a few pointers on that subject,' grinned Sunderland.

'I'm sure you could, Sergeant, but I reckon the good doctor is more concerned with the causes of criminal behaviour rather than how to spot a snout at a hundred paces.'

'You may be right.'

'But Sexton spent a lot of time interviewing Northcote at Newfield House. He must have got to know him very well. God help us, he should be able to give us some inkling of where the bastard is now and what his plans are.'

'You would hope so,' said Sunderland without much conviction.

* * *

Dr Francis Sexton's surgery was in Bedford Row, a smart thoroughfare situated between High Holborn and Theobalds Road. As Sunderland pulled the car up outside, he asked, 'Do you want me to stay out here, sir?'

David shook his head, 'No, come in with me. Four ears and two brains, eh? What one of us might miss, the other should pick up. At least we can dissect things afterwards.'

A rather matronly secretary showed the two policemen

into Dr Sexton's consulting room. He rose magisterially from behind his desk and shook Llewellyn's hand.

'I take it you've not caught him, then?' he said easily as he gestured that the two men should take the seats opposite the desk.

He was a tall man, somewhere in his late forties with a prominent nose and grizzled hair, shot with silver strands. He was, thought David, someone who was used to being in command and at complete ease with himself. He was dressed in a well-cut grey double breasted suit and had a relaxed and confident manner. The inspector gazed down at his own old baggy suit and scuffed shoes and immediately felt awkward.

'No, we haven't caught him – but I'm afraid that he has already committed murder.'

Sexton pursed his lips and nodded. 'Sadly, that does not surprise me. The man has an inner compulsion to kill...'

'And then eat his victims.'

'Yes. In hospital, drugs can sublimate the condition, keep it in check to some extent, but now he is away from any kind of control or restraint his desires will be... unfettered.'

'Why does he do it?' asked Sunderland.

'That is the big question I was trying to answer by talking to him. Cannibalism – the eating of human flesh – has been with us since the dawn of time, but it is mostly a cultural phenomenon. It was often based on the belief that by eating one's enemy you inherit his power. Humans have also indulged in the practice as a means of self preservation. In many non-European countries, it was not regarded as a sin or a crime to consume human flesh. For example in the Aztec or Mayan culture cannibalism was reserved for royalty. After a ritual human sacrifice to their Gods, they would feast upon their victims. However, in Ralph Northcote's case, he kills purely for pleasure and celebrates his act by devouring part of the flesh of his victim.'

'For pleasure?' said David.

'Yes.'

'Then the fellow is mad.'

'From our perspective, yes.'

'But ours is the sane one.'

Sexton gave the inspector an indulgent smile. 'But who's to say that our perspective is the correct one – the only acceptable one? Northcote just views the world from a different hilltop. As a psychiatrist I have to take the position that the mind controls the man – not morals, laws or customs, which in essence are all artificial codes imposed on us by exterior forces, created by society. I was trying to unlock the door in order to find out why his view of the world differed from the majority.'

'It sounds as you feel sorry for him.'

'In a way, I do. Imagine yourself trapped within a psyche that was vastly different from the accepted norm and there was nothing you could do about it. It is so much easier to give in to our natural urges than fight them. We do it all the time.'

'Natural urges.' David scowled.

'To Northcote they are natural. Do you smoke, Inspector?'

'Yes.'

'It's bad for the health, you know.'

'I know.'

'Have you tried to give up?'

'From time to time.'

'But you haven't succeeded.'

'No.'

'No doubt the temptation to light up was too strong. You gave way to your natural urges despite the fact that you knew you'd be better off not smoking. The pleasure you receive from tobacco is greater than the concerns you have for your health. The principle is the same. Northcote has given up all attempts to stifle his appetite for murder and blood.'

'I think perhaps we are wandering a little way from the purpose of this visit. Whatever weird psychological processes control Ralph Northcote, I represent the mainstream law and order of this country. In my eyes he is a violent murderer and it's my task to find him and stop him before he takes any more lives.'

Sexton nodded urbanely. 'I understand. And you think I can help.'

'Well, I hope so. You have spent quite a lot of time with him. I would have thought that he must have given you some inkling about his plans. You got inside his head... knew how he thought.'

'I was beginning to understand some of his rationale, but I'm not able to think like him, if that is what you are suggesting.'

'If not think like him – guess what he might do next. Guess what his plans are.'

'I doubt it. He is a very cunning man. I must admit that he had me completely fooled. I thought he trusted me – saw in me someone who at least could understand and sympathise with his mania.'

'Sympathise?' David could not keep the shock out of his voice.

'In the scientific sense, of course. It is true that in order to gain his trust I did pretend to empathise with his cravings. In this way he felt safe to confide in me his innermost thoughts.'

'And...?' There was a note of irritation in Llewellyn's voice. He was getting a little tired of Sexton's mumbo jumbo sophistry. It was as though all this psycho-jargon was a smokescreen. This fellow knew something. Llewellyn had no idea what but he was determined to find out.

'Well, I learned a fair bit about Northcote's biography and his early encounters with the tasting of flesh. I began to fathom what triggered off the overwhelming urge to kill and feast.'

David groaned inwardly. The phrase 'to kill and feast': it was a conscious, flashy, overly-clever construct which glamorised the subject describing it in a facile way. No doubt, he thought, Sexton will use it as the title for his book.

'And what was that? What was this trigger?'

'I believe it was connected with sexual arousal. Instead of the need for sexual intercourse and the physical and mental release that this brings, Northcote transferred this natural desire to…'

'An urge to kill and feast,' added David pointedly.

'Yes.'

'To learn all this, Northcote must have trusted you.'

'Yes… to some extent. Not enough to reveal any plans to escape, if that's what you're hinting at. Well, that would have been foolish. After all I was his means to freedom. I was certainly kept in the dark about that.'

'But he must have talked about his desire to get out of that place.' It was Sunderland who made this observation.

'Not really. He seemed resigned to his fate. I suppose that fact alone should have alerted me to the notion that he was planning something.'

'Could you explain what you mean?' asked David, unable to keep the irritation out of his voice.

'Incarceration, drugs, therapy can never fully quell the innate cravings of a patient like Northcote. The desire is forever there, lurking in the shadows. It may be sedated for a time but it is never eradicated. The fact that Northcote appeared placid and in a state of acceptance should have warned me that he was keeping something back from me.'

'And you've only realised this now?'

'Since I was coshed on the head in Newfield House, yes.'

David sighed heavily. This was going nowhere and certainly Sexton was making no real effort to help. He was wrapped up in his own esoteric psychobabble world and the practical realities of catching a vicious murderer did not seem to concern him in the slightest. He decided to try a different tack with this obtuse medic.

'Dr Sexton, if you were me, a policeman trying to trace Ralph Northcote, what would you do?'

Sexton seemed amused by the question and stared into space for some seconds before responding. 'Do you know, inspector, I really have no idea. As I say, he is a cunning fellow. Do not mistake his mania for overall madness. He has a cool, clever rational mind and he would have no difficulty in becoming invisible in this city. Actually that is something that is quite easy to do these days what with the black out and so many damaged properties where a fugitive could easily hang out without being detected.'

'In the course of your chats, did Northcote mention any old colleagues, friends – even enemies?'

The psychiatrist shook his head. 'His past life was a closed book to him. I don't suppose he could have made his way to his old house, could he?'

'It no longer exists. It was pulled down. There's nothing there now.'

Sexton gave an elegant shrug of his well-tailored shoulders. 'I'm sorry. I have nothing else to suggest. Northcote is now both the hunter and the hunted: there is no template for such a role. Certainly not one that I could fathom. I am sorry.'

* * *

'That man is an arrogant, supercilious, irritating, pompous smug twit,' growled Inspector David Llewellyn as he slumped into the passenger seat. 'No, I take that back. He's not a twit. He had no intention of helping us and he made that patently obvious.'

'Why do you think that is, sir?' said Sergeant Sunderland turning the key in the ignition and revving the engine.

'I don't know. Perhaps he didn't want to get his hands dirty with police work. Perhaps his sympathies for Northcote were genuine and he's pleased the bugger's escaped.'

'Really!'

'Well, no not really, I suppose. But during all those visits Northcote must have said something – something however innocent or trivial that could give us some sort of clue as to where he's hiding out. One thing is for certain, I don't go along with Sexton's notion that he's hiding in some bombed out building. He's found somewhere much smarter than that. I'm sure of it.'

'How do you make that out?'

'When he killed that girl, he didn't touch her purse – he left her money alone which suggests that he has sufficient for his needs. If that is the case, where has the dosh come from? He has secured a supply from somewhere.'

'Maybe a secret stash that he hid before he was captured.'

'That's a bit far fetched. He's been locked away for eight years. That kind of perspicacity would be remarkable. And then there's the murder itself. It's obvious that Northcote used proper medical equipment to cut up and dissect the body. Where'd he get them from?'

'I could check if there have been any thefts of such stuff from hospitals or surgeries in the last few days.'

'Yeah, you do that, but I reckon you'll get a nil result. My hunch is that our friend Northcote is being harboured, given refuge by some twisted sod who sympathises with him.'

'Sympathises?' Sunderland's voice rose an octave.

'Yes,' said David thoughtfully, lighting a cigarette. 'Sympathises. There's that word again.'

* * *

Back in his office, Francis Sexton was also smoking and idly watching the smoke spiral fade while his mind lingered over the interview he'd just had with Inspector Llewellyn and his lackey. In retrospect Sexton believed that he had handled it badly. He had been too smooth, too unhelpful. He'd certainly been in control and had effectively deflected each of the policeman's questions, giving absolutely nothing away but in doing so he had obviously irritated him. That, Sexton knew, had been a foolish thing to do. He really should have thrown Llewellyn a titbit to chew on to send him off on a wild goose chase; a false clue that indicated that he was trying to help the police instead of being apparently indifferent to their investigation.

Now the policemen had gone away, frustrated and annoyed with him. He cursed softly. He had been so pleased with his smooth performance at the time that he had been unaware of the damage he was doing. Had he, by his mannered performance, aroused their suspicions? Surely not. But the thought lingered like a dark cloud.

SEVENTEEN

Before turning in for the night, I'd sat up in bed and read through the file on Bruce Horsefield, the true identity of Lance Corporal Marshall but had learned nothing of any significance. Well, nothing that could give me a lead. It was a familiar scenario: unruly kid developed into a teenage hoodlum, petty crimes and then in 1936 he'd tried his hand at holding up a jewellers' shop. It was an amateurish attempt, albeit with a shooter, and he was chased down the street and caught. He was gaoled for five years but released early in order to join the army to fight for his country. Within months he had deserted and disappeared. He was an only child, brought up by his widowed mother. She was still alive, but claims not to have seen him since he went in the army. Her house had been searched and initially a watch had been put on it to no avail. End of story.

With a heavy sigh, I switched out the lights and then just as my head hit the pillow, a thought came to me. It was nothing to do with Horsefield – well not directly – but it amazed me why I hadn't thought of it before. I lay in the dark smiling for some time before I slipped into a dreamless sleep.

The next morning I was up bright and early and out on the streets before nine. I had my revolver with me, weighing down the pocket of my raincoat. It is rare that I carry a weapon. I'm not keen on the beasts, especially after what one malfunctioning rifle did to my eye, but in this instance it was a case of forewarned being forearmed. I had worked out in my little brain that Malcolm Salter was not only on the run from the police but also from his partner in crime, Bruce Horsefield. For some reason they had split up, probably some argument over the spoils of the bank robbery and he was desperately trying to lie low so neither Horsefield could find him nor the coppers could feel his collar. He'd kipped out at his mother's place until her death – that was still a bit of a mystery to me. Then he'd holed up at Mrs Booth's boarding house, until I turned up on the doorstep and he turned nasty with a pistol. Where might he go next?

Well, I had an idea.

I knocked once more on the shiny knocker of Mrs Frances Coulson's bijou bungalow. As I did so, the door partially swung open and there was no one on the other side. A little warning voice in my brain went, 'Oh-oh!' I knew what it meant. Experience has taught me that when you go to a door you anticipate will be locked but it isn't, you usually can expect trouble.

I stepped over the threshold and pulled out my gun. 'Hello,' I called down the hallway.

There was no reply.

Something was up. Something was very up.

And then I heard it. A faint sound, rather like a groan. There it was again. It was a groan – and it was coming from the sitting room.

Cautiously, I entered the room. The tidy little parlour was in a state of disarray. One of the chairs had been overturned and many of the ornaments were lying haphazardly on the floor. It was obvious that there had been some sort of struggle in here. This deduction was further strengthened when I observed Mrs Frances Coulson stretched out on the couch, her left arm hanging limply to the floor while she clutched a wound to her forehead with her right. Blood veined its way down her pale face making her resemble some kind of bizarre clown. At first she wasn't aware of my presence. I knelt down beside her and touched her shoulder gently.

'Mrs Coulson,' I said softly.

Her eyes rolled open and with a sharp grimace she turned her head in my direction.

'Who... are you?'

'It's Johnny Hawke... the private detective.'

Her eyelids fluttered and then closed. 'Oh. You.'

'What happened?'

'I was attacked. He... came for Malcolm.'

Here voice was raspy and lazy like that of a drunk.

'Malcolm Salter. He's been here.'

'His last refuge. But ... he found him. He came for him.'

'Who?

'The man. The man that did this to me.'

'Which man?'

Mrs Coulson's brow creased with irritation and her eyes flickered open again. 'Horsefield. He came for the money.'

The money. Like a rusty machine that had just been serviced and well-oiled, suddenly all the cogs slipped into place and began whirring with increased efficiency. Now it all became clear to me. Or most of it, at least.

'I told him Malcolm wasn't here, but he didn't believe me,' Mrs Coulson rambled on. 'So, he hit me. Broke my skull.'

'You'll be all right,' I said without any knowledge or conviction that this would be the case. At least I knew her skull wasn't broken. She had a bad cut and her dignity had been bruised. 'Let me get you a glass of water.'

'A glass of water... yes. Put some gin in it too, would you?'

I reckon she'd survive.

I got her the water – without the gin. I didn't want to waste precious time searching for booze in the kitchen.

'Where have Malcolm and Horsefield gone now?' I asked

after helping to prop Mrs Coulson up into a sitting position on the sofa and handing her the glass of water, which she clasped unsteadily with both hands.

She took a gulp from the glass and then turned a puzzled face to me. 'What did you say?'

'Malcolm and Horsefield – the man who attacked you – where have they gone?'

At the mention of the attack, Mrs Coulson's fingers wandered towards the wound again. 'They've gone to get the money, of course.'

'Where?' I tried to keep the frustration and eagerness out of my voice, but I feel I failed.

Mrs Coulson looked at me crossly as though I was an idiot. 'To Victoria Station. Malcolm said that he'd put the money in a left luggage locker for safe keeping.'

'How long ago did they leave?'

'How the hell do I know? I've been attacked. I don't know how long I've been lying here, suffering.' She took another drink. 'Hey,' she said, 'there's no gin in this.'

As I hurried for the door, I noticed the clock that had been on the mantelpiece lying on the tiled hearth, no doubt where it had fallen during the struggle. The glass face was cracked and the hands had stopped at ten to ten. I glanced at my watch. That was twenty minutes ago. Crikey, I had only just missed them. I reckon they had about a fifteen-minute lead on me.

In a trice I was out of the house and racing up the road in search of a taxi. I felt no guilt in leaving the wounded Mrs Coulson to her own devices. She was a tough old bird and I'm sure that she'd summon up enough strength to get to the gin bottle and comfort herself that way.

Despite the coolness of the morning, I had worked up quite a sweat before I managed to secure a taxi. They were thin on the ground in suburbia.

'Victoria Station,' I yelled as I jumped inside.' As fast as you can. It's a matter of life and death,' I added for dramatic effort.

The cabbie gave a brief smile. 'Yeah, it always is mate,' he muttered and slammed his foot down hard on the accelerator causing the cab to leap forward and for me to be thrown with some force back into my seat. The fellow had taken me at my word.

As we travelled, I tried to assemble my thoughts and build a clear scenario of this troubled affair. I was making some assumptions certainly, but they were all based on things I knew for certain. Here's how I read the riddle at that time. Malcolm Salter and Bruce Horsefield – i.e. Lance Corporal Marshall – had absconded from the army and formed a criminal partnership. Horsefield had experience in breaking the law, albeit a fairly unsuccessful one, and probably gave Salter a crash course in the mechanics of stealing. No doubt they carried out a few small robberies and then went for the big time with the bank job in Chelmsford. It seemed to me that it was at this time that Malcolm got greedy and somehow absconded with the loot. Big mistake. Horsefield had form for being a violent beggar and certainly would not take this lightly.

I reckoned that Salter had turned up at his mother's place intending to hide out there while the heat died down. But Horsefield had tracked him down and he only managed to get away before his old partner came to call, finding the cupboard bare, as it were. Horsefield took it out on the old woman, hanging the poor old soul. Probably it was done partly as revenge and partly as a warning to Salter. He made it look like suicide so the police wouldn't be suspicious of her death, but he knew Malcolm would know the truth.

Salter went on the run and that's where I came in,

tracking him down to Mrs Booth's lodging house. Actually, I did him a favour for in giving me the slip, he did the same to Horsefield who was no doubt hot on his heels. As a last resort he went to Auntie Susan for shelter. I didn't know to what extent she was party to all this, but she certainly wasn't a whited sepulchre. Now Horsefield's got him and is dragging him to where he secreted the loot – a left-luggage locker at Victoria Station. I had no doubt that when Horsefield had got his hands on the cash, he would have no compunctions about killing his traitorous partner.

Unless I could get there in time.

And getting there in time was proving a problem.

In the good old days – i.e. before the war – travelling around London was fairly easy. Of course, there were the usual snarl ups on the road at busy spots but, in general, journeys went rather smoothly without any serious delay. And then came the Luftwaffe causing all kinds of havoc: bombed buildings spilling across the thoroughfares, water and gas mains destroyed, rubble and debris blocking roads, craters causing diversions, a whole catalogue of obstructions which hindered the swift and easy passage from place to place.

While my cabbie was driving as fast as he could we did not seem to be making much progress. Once in the city, there were so many detours, down this back street, up that road, to just get a little bit further on the direct route. The only consolation was that Horsefield and Salter would have suffered the same problems. I assumed they had gone by road. If they had taken the underground, the odds on me getting there at the same time or even before them shortened. There were several changes on route and tube trains ran infrequently during the day between rush-hour times.

We jerked to a halt and the cabbie suddenly peeped his

horn ferociously. We had got stuck behind a horse and cart, the driver of which seemed oblivious of other road users.

'Deaf bastard!' snarled the cabbie and leaned out of his window. 'Shift your arse, mate,' he yelled.

The driver of the cart was indeed deaf or impervious to such urging and maintained his snail-like pace.

With a grunt of anger, the cabbie wrenched the wheel to the right and mounted the pavement, while at the same time stabbing his hand down firmly on the horn to produce a loud and continuous blare of warning. Pedestrians scattered, but the cart trotted on calmly. With an extra surge of speed, the cab rocketed past the cart and we shuddered back down onto the road and continued our journey at speed.

The cabbie said nothing to me, but I could hear him chuckling to himself.

Soon the great edifice of Victoria station hove into view. What, I wondered, would I find inside.

EIGHTEEN

He was used to pain. He could handle pain. In many ways pain was pleasurable. And in this instance it was necessary. He tugged even harder but forced himself not to wince, despite the fierce sharp electric shock waves that shot up his arm. The flesh was scraping off now. Shredding like thin slices of uncooked beef.

He tugged again and this time, he could not suppress a cry and a curse. But as he cursed, he tugged even harder, the blood welling over the cold metal of the handcuff.

Now he was wracked with pain and wanted to curl up in a ball and sob. But he knew he couldn't. He had gone this far. He had to go all the way. All the excruciating way. Before making another almighty effort, he gazed down at his damaged hand. It was almost down to the bone by the knuckles and the rest was raw flesh which glistened in the shadowy light.

Taking a deep breath, he bellowed loudly, bellowed until his lungs hurt, hoping the noise and the discomfort would help to mask the pain of one more violent effort. Contracting his fingers as much as he could, he wrenched his damaged hand further through the metal hoop of the handcuff. Without waiting for the full extent of the agony this caused to register in his brain, he did it again. Flames shot up before his eyes, bright red and yellow and his whole body rippled with agony.

But he was free.

He was free.

He looked down at the bloody mess that was his hand and tied to flex his fingers. Reluctantly they obeyed. Ralph Northcote smiled and then fell back on the bed in a dead faint.

When he awoke some twenty minutes later, he first became conscious of the throbbing ache in his right hand. Memory of his actions seem to aid the pain and as he sat up, it grew in intensity. Strangely, he smiled, his dry lips pulling back across his teeth in a feral grin. He could cope. The pain would lessen in time. The main thing was that he had not damaged the function of the hand – and that he was free. He swung his legs over the side of the bed and tried to stand up. He did so for a few moments and then collapsed back down again. He was very weak and a little light headed due to a lack of sustenance. After a few moments, he tried again and remained upright this time. His first tasks were to bandage his hand and obtain some food and water. Then he could prepare to make good his escape.

Haltingly at first, he walked to the cellar door and with his good hand, he managed to pull it open. He sneered. Sexton had been so confident that his prisoner could not escape he hadn't even bothered to lock the door.

Slowly in a shambling manner he made his way upstairs into the main body of the house and located the kitchen. In the larder he found a pork pie and a few sausages. He devoured them savagely, washed down with water. Then he attended to his hand, running it gently under the tap before using a tea towel as a makeshift bandage. In the sitting room, he found Sexton's cigarette case on the mantelpiece, the initials F S engraved on the top. Extracting a cigarette, he sat in one of the armchairs and enjoyed a smoke. As he stubbed the tab end out on the arm of the chair, he smiled again. From now on things were going to go his way.

For hours, while he had lain on that filthy bed in the cellar, he had planned in meticulous detail what he would do when he got free and now he set about doing it. Only the strange geography of the house hindered him slightly. Upstairs, in the bathroom, he found a medicine cabinet and he treated his wound, dabbing Dettol onto it, and crying out in pain as he did so, and then dressing it with a crepe bandage. The cabinet also offered up a treasure: a small neat case containing a set of surgical instruments. He opened the case and admired the bright metal tools of his trade and his hobby. They glistened pleasingly in the natural light.

'Excellent,' murmured Northcote, stroking the leather case. 'That eliminates one of my perceived hurdles.'

This lucky find seemed to increase his energy levels. With enthusiasm, he washed, combed his hair and shaved using Sexton's razor, an act that gave him great pleasure.

Moving into the main bedroom, he raided the wardrobe, taking a smart brown suit and a cream shirt and tie. Then came the shoes. He chose a nice pair of sturdy brogues. Sexton had small feet, but cramped toes were small inconvenience compared with the throbbing discomfort of his injured hand. Every time he thought of it, he moved his fingers to reassure himself that they were still working. He also found a small stash of notes and coins in the bedside drawer – around fifteen pounds. Northcote scooped it up and slipped it in his pocket.

He selected a smart overcoat, something dark and discreet, and checked himself out in the wardrobe mirror. He looked almost human. The face was ghostly white and haggard, the eyes bloodshot and the posture a little hunched, but he reckoned he would pass unnoticed in a crowd.

He was prepared to face the world once more, but before he did, there was just one more thing he had to do.

He moved back into the sitting room and picked up the

cigarette case and slipped it into his pocket.

Now he was ready.

Within minutes, he was walking down the street, away from Sexton's house and towards freedom and the city of London.

NINETEEN

I paid off the cabbie with a healthy tip. His kerb-mounting routine was beyond the call of duty, and without his ingenuity and bravado, I would, no doubt, be still stuck behind that crawling horse and cart.

I entered the portals of Victoria Station, not really knowing what was going to happen to me here. A wave of noise washed over me: a multitude of echoey voices floating round the great domed structure, built like some great industrial cathedral. The place was crowded, passengers of all sizes, shapes and ages criss-crossed and interwove with each other like a moving canvas of drab colours.

I knew where the left luggage lockers were situated, down the side of Platform One and headed in that direction. I moved as quickly as I could, fighting against a tide of folk rolling the other way. The whole of London seemed to be squeezing their way past me. At last I reached Platform One, my hand clasped firmly on my revolver. I peered down towards the lockers and the various individuals hovering around them like expectant bees around the proverbial honey pot. I'd come face to face with Salter in the flesh, so I thought that I would recognise him, but Horsefield was only a face on an old sepia photograph. There was, of course, his hat, the large grey felt fedora.

And there it was! Large as life, bobbing towards me.

My heart began to race. I knew now that a confrontation was inevitable and certainly one of us would get hurt. I just had to make sure that it was not me. I pushed forward towards the hat, while at the same time trying to see if Malcolm Salter was accompanying it. It did not seem so.

The jostling crowd seemed to coagulate as I neared that distinctive titfer and then suddenly there was a gap into which I was propelled and faced the owner of the hat. It wasn't him. It wasn't Horsefield. It was a gentle-faced fellow well into his seventies who was having great trouble hauling a large brown case along the platform. Under normal circumstances I would have stopped and offered assistance, but these were not normal circumstances.

I squeezed past the old fellow and moved further down the platform, feeling that now I was on a fool's errand. The row of green metal lockers stretched for about twelve feet and about half a dozen passengers were installing or extracting luggage or parcels when I arrived. None of them was Salter or Horsefield. It looked like I was too late and my hopes of bringing this investigation to a swift conclusion were well and truly dashed. With sloping shoulders of defeat, I loitered by the lockers for a few minutes and turned to make my way back up the platform.

And then I saw it again. That hat! But it wasn't the same one. Not unless the old chap with the big case had turned around and was making his way up the platform now. But no, this hat certainly belonged to Horsefield for there was his thin sallow face beneath the brim and at his side was my old sparring partner, Malcolm Salter who looked as cheerful as a fat turkey on Christmas Eve. He was almost being dragged along by Felt Hat Horsefield, whose face was set in a ferocious scowl, his hand thrust deep in his raincoat pocket. Unless I was mistaken that unpleasant bulge indicated there was a gun in there, a sinister little persuader.

As soon as I'd clocked them, I turned around to hide my face and moved to the side of the platform by the Gentlemen's lavatories, and waited until they had passed me. Then I turned and followed them.

On reaching the lockers, I could see Horsefield snapping instructions to Salter, who very slowly retrieved a key from his wallet and passed it to his companion. Horsefield refused to take it and made Salter open the locker himself. Obviously he was taking no chances for Salter to do a bunk. Slowly, he opened the locker door and withdrew a dark maroon holdall. Horsefield snatched it from him and uttered some instructions and the two of them turned and began to retrace their steps. I turned sideways and appeared to be reading one of the railway notices on the wall as they went by me. They turned and disappeared into the gents' lavatories. I reckoned that Horsefield was just going to check that the money was indeed in the maroon holdall. And then what? It seemed to me there was only one likely outcome. He would shoot Salter.

* * *

Taking a deep breath, I entered the lavatories a few moments later. At first sight, it was empty. There was no one there at all. It was as though the two men had disappeared into thin air. Had I been tricked? Had it all been a performance for my benefit? But no. I head a rustling noise from one of the cubicles and bending down I could see two sets of feet visible below the door. I pressed the door gently; it was locked. Without hesitation, I stood back and lifting up my leg I rammed it hard with my size nines. It sprang open and there were cries from within and to my horror the sound of a gun shot.

Horsefield spilled out, clasping the holdall to his chest with one hand and holding the smoking gun with the other. Behind him I could see the body of Malclom Salter. He was slumped on the lavatory, his head down on his chest.

On seeing me, Horsefield thrust the gun in my direction. I could tell from his distracted glances that things had evolved too fast for him to realise exactly what was happening. He had no idea who I was or what I wanted. For all he knew, I could be a chap in desperate need of a lavatory cubicle. I took advantage of his hesitation. With the gun still in my raincoat pocket, I shot him in the leg. He went down immediately with a cry. For some reason, I glanced down at my coat and saw the awful hole and scorchmarks that disfigured it. Damn!

I should not have been so lax. A bullet whistled past my ear and I stumbled backward in surprise. Horsefield had staggered to his feet and was edging his way to the exit. His leg was bleeding through his trousers, but I reckoned he was not badly hurt. Probably the bullet had skimmed the flesh causing only a slight wound. Well, I hadn't exactly been in a position to aim with any great accuracy. He paused in his flight and I could see that he was ready to fire again. I knew that this time he wouldn't miss. With a speed I didn't know I possessed, I dived into the cubicle, almost landing on Malcolm Salter's lap. He sighed and his body shifted sideways. He wasn't dead then, I thought. And neither was I.

I waited a moment before I and my gun appeared around the edge of the cubicle. There was no reaction. Horsefield had gone.

I ran out onto the platform, glancing both ways. A wild array of jostling passengers met my gaze both ways. But again, the hat caught my eye. There he was. There was Horsefield. I spied him some hundred yards ahead of me, racing – well, hobbling – in a speedy fashion down towards the end of the platform, away from the main concourse. I set out after him.

TWENTY

Peter should have been at school and he did feel a slight pang of guilt about playing truant, but he reckoned that his bunking off was in a good cause. At least, he had convinced himself this was the case. He was determined to follow in Johnny's footsteps and become a detective when he started work and his plan today was in a sense a trial excursion to see how successful he would be in this pursuit. With a bit of luck he may well help Johnny to bring his case to a close. That would be a real feather in his cap and convince Johnny of his talents as an investigator. Well, it was worth a try anyway.

And he had dressed for the part. He had adapted his school clothes – ditching the cap and tie and slipping on his scruffy playing out trousers – while messing his hair and smearing a little dirt on his face so that he looked like a scruffy urchin of whom no one would take any notice. A scruffy urchin of the type, he assumed, would be roaming around the streets of Houndsditch. So successful was his 'disguise' that the conductor wouldn't let him board the bus until he had provided evidence of his ability to pay. He was not in the least bit embarrassed by this challenge as the 'real' Peter would have been.

Peter had never been to Houndsditch before, but as a student of crime he knew that it wasn't very far from Whitechapel, the scene of the Jack the Ripper murders and the violent Sydney Street Siege in 1911. It was a scruffy down at heel district, but most places in London were these days: the dust and debris of war invaded all areas of the city. Peter was well aware that this was a bit of a wild goose chase but he reasoned even wild geese get caught sometimes. He had studied the picture of Bruce Horsefield from the paper and his description. He knew from Johnny that this fellow was in the habit of wearing a grey felt hat, almost like the cowboys wore in the films. Houndsditch was his home territory. Of course it had been reported in the papers that the police had visited his mother and she claimed that she hadn't seen 'neither hide nor hair of the blighter since he joined up.' They had searched her house and, of course, found nothing; but that was not to say that Marshall hadn't been waiting until the police went away. Of course, Peter realised that they would probably have put a man on to watch the house, but a clever criminal should be able to enter and leave his old home without being seen. But what brought Peter to Houndsditch was not just this thin possibility but his belief that if Horsefield was in hiding, what better place to do it than in his old manor. There would be cronies here who would help him, shelter him and keep the rozzers off his back.

Peter's plan was to patrol the streets hoping to pick up a clue or, better still, catch sight of Horsefield.

But first he had to indulge in a little dramatic interlude.

He made his way to 25 Napier Grove. The home of Mrs Horsefield.

Old Mother Riley opened the door. Or so it seemed to Peter. Standing on the threshold was a bony old woman with high cheekbones, a prominent nose and fierce eyes which were fixed permanently in the accusative mode. This vision before him was the epitome of the music hall character he'd seen in a few films and had a two-page spread in one of his favourite comics. Her arms from the elbow down were bare and flapped like a trapped seagull in true Mother Riley fashion. The impression that this harridan was indeed the famous comic washerwoman was completed by the tartan shawl draped around her shoulders.

'Yes?' she bleated without ceremony.

'I'm sorry to trouble you, Mrs, but could you let me have a glass of water? I've sort of come over a bit faint. I… er... didn't have no breakfast. Sort of dizzy.' He rocked backwards and forwards on his heels as if to demonstrate his 'dizzy' state.

The woman peered over his shoulder into the street beyond as though she expected to see others there all wanting a glass of water – or perhaps something more sinister.

'You're not from round here?' she croaked.

'No, Mrs, I'm on my way to visit my grandad. Just a glass of water, please.' He rocked on his feet once more and rolled his eyes to add further icing to his little dramatic cake. He had carefully rehearsed this performance the night before.

'Don't you go passing out on my doorstep,' the old crone said.

'I'll try not to,' he replied faintly and gave an extra roll of the eyes.

'All right. A glass of water. Then you get off to your grandad's.'

'Thank you.' He made a move to step inside, but a bony hand on his chest held him back.

'You wait here. I'll bring a glass out to you.'

Peter hadn't expected this. He had thought that he would be invited in to the kitchen. He wanted to case the joint. The plan was failing. The woman, who Peter assumed was Mrs Horsefield, retreated down the hall and disappeared. He took a few steps into the house and gazed down the hallway, hoping some clue would leap out at him. There was a coat rack at the far end with several items of clothing hanging from it. Sadly they all appeared to be those worn by ladies. There was no grey felt hat dangling from one of the hooks.

'Hey, I told you to stay where you were.'

Old Mother Riley had appeared again carrying a glass of water.

'Sorry.' Peter retreated on to the top step.

'Get this down you and then be off with you. I ain't no bleedin' hospital.' She thrust the glass at Peter, spilling some of the contents down his jacket.

Without a word, he drank the water. It was cold and salty.

'Thank you,' he said, as the bony hand snatched the glass from him. Then the door slammed in his face.

Wiping away the drips of water from around his mouth with his sleeve, Peter walked away from 25 Napier Grove hugely disappointed. His dramatic ploy had produced nothing at all – no evidence that Bruce Horsefield was hiding out at home or, indeed, any clue as to where he might be. The plan, for which he had such high hopes, had been a failure.

Thoroughly despondent, he walked a little while up the street and then sat on a low wall to ponder what to do next. He had been so sure that he would be invited in to Widow Horsefield's kitchen where he would spot some clue that indicated that her son Bruce was hiding out there – two places set at the kitchen table, a pair of men's shoes in the hearth, a jacket draped on the back of a chair or even the grey felt hat hung behind the door – but nothing. This failure was completely unexpected and he had not thought beyond it.

After wallowing in his disappointment for ten minutes or so, he shrugged his shoulders, realising that as a detective one must overcome setbacks all the time. Johnny would certainly not be beaten by such an outcome. He would have to persevere.

Houndsditch was Horsefield's stamping ground and it seemed to Peter that a man on the run, like a wounded animal, would return to his own lair. If not his family home, some gaff in the vicinity. So, he would pound the streets, pound the scruffy streets of Houndsditch, in the hope of... something.

And so hauling himself to his feet, Peter began his trek. It was now mid-morning and the streets were fairly empty: those who had jobs were at work, night shift fellows were in bed and housewives were inside doing what housewives do. In one of the streets there were a few kids who like Peter were bunking off school and were involved in an impromptu game of cricket. He hung around and watched and waited and after retrieving the ball from the gutter a couple of times, managed to get himself involved in the game. This led to idle chatter which at length he was able to swing his way. Eventually, he felt comfortable to ask if they knew the local villain who had been in the papers for robbing a bank. A geezer called Horsefield. The query met with blank stares. Even when he described Horsefield, including the detail of his felt cowboy hat, the stares remained blank. Another dead end. Realising that there was nothing to be gained from this particular cricket match, he quickly dropped out and began to mooch his way along another street.

At lunchtime he called in a café for a mug of tea and a piece of cake. He gazed around at the customers, mostly folk on their own, pale-faced and lost in thought. They all looked respectable and sad. No sign of a felt hat anywhere.

The afternoon was spent drearily tramping around streets of the area once more. He passed the Horsefield house again and even scouted around the lane at the back to no avail. Tired and fed up, Peter reckoned he'd better go home. It was nearly five o'clock and he needed to be back for tea or the Horner sisters would get worried. And anyway, it had been a futile mission. Nothing was going to present itself to him now.

But he was wrong.

TWENTY-ONE

When Horsefield reached the end of the platform, he dropped over the edge and began to cross the railway tracks. I was tempted to shoot at him, but I knew that I was no Wyatt-Earp type sharp shooter and I was probably too far away from the target to be successful. However, unlike my quarry, I was an able-bodied fellow – no wound to hinder me – and I reckoned I could soon catch up with him.

In copycat fashion, I slipped over the edge of the platform too and began picking my way across the tracks. By now Horsefield had progressed past the end of the next platform and further out, beyond the confines of the canopy of the station. In turning to see how far I was behind him, he stumbled and fell full length with a sharp cry. Now was my chance. But it was foiled by the appearance of a goods train that seemed to loom out of thin air and shudder slowly past me on the line between Horsefield and myself. The clanking, thundering monster rattled by at a snail's pace while I stood impotently immobile, unable to move or indeed see my man.

When the train had passed in a cloud of gritty smoke, I peered ahead. There was no sign of Horsefield. 'Damn,' I cried out loud and set off across the tracks again in the direction my quarry had been heading. Every so often I saw a splash of red on the iron or the sleepers: blood from his wound. I stopped for a moment and gazed around me. I suddenly realised how bizarre this situation was. Here I was standing in the middle of a tracery of railway lines searching for a wounded man who was escaping with a fortune in stolen notes. I had a vision of myself as viewed from above – a solitary human figure staggering across a series of interconnecting silver rails like some vision created by Salvador Dali or some other crazy surrealist painter.

My reverie was interrupted by the sound of a shot. On instinct I dropped to my knees. One shot, the bullet pinging onto the rails some yards ahead of me. I scanned the scene before me: signals, static rolling stock and those hypnotic silver rails sliding off into the distance – but there was no sign of Horsefield. Where had the shot come from?

And then I spied him. Or rather his legs. I saw a movement behind one of the goods trucks some hundred yards away to my right. In the gap between the wagon and the ground, I saw two legs shifting slightly.

Adopting a low crouch which that fellow from Notre Dame would have been proud of, I made my way as quickly as I could towards the wagon while keeping my eyes focused on those legs. As I grew nearer, I saw Horsefield move to the corner of the truck and peer around the corner. On seeing the loping figure bearing down on him, he fired again. As he did so, I threw myself sideways. Just in time, as it happened, for the bullet thudded into the sleeper where seconds earlier I had been crouching.

Now the legs disappeared altogether. Maybe the devil was climbing up the side in order to get onto the roof for a better view. Certainly, I'd be a much easier target from up there.

I ran the rest of the distance and on reaching the goods wagon I pressed my body to its side. I listened carefully for any sound which may give me a clue as to Horsefield's actual whereabouts. Had he clambered on to the roof or was he just around the other side clinging on? I could hear nothing, but as I moved stealthily towards the right corner of the truck, I heard the sounds of raised voices. I turned quickly and saw in the distance behind me, three men racing in my direction. One was a uniformed policeman, and the other two appeared to be railway officials, guards or something like that. They were raising their hands in the air and shouting loudly. I couldn't hear what they were saying, but I caught the word 'Stop!' It was clear they were some kind of posse and by their demeanour, it seemed I was their quarry.

I had stared at them too long for suddenly I was conscious of a shadow and then a presence near me. I turned quickly but too late. I saw Horsefield. I saw Horsefield with his arm raised high. I saw Horsefield bring the butt of the gun down towards me. I saw blackness.

* * *

When I awoke, I found myself lying on a small utility bed with screens around me. As I tried to sit up, a hand grenade went off in my head. I groaned. The screens parted and a young woman in a nurse's outfit appeared and smiled gently.

'So you have returned to the land of the living, eh?'

It was a pleasant voice, low in register and with an accent. Middle European. I guessed that, but I had no idea where I was.

'Where am I?' My voice escaped like a tired mole into the daylight.

'You are in the First Aid room at Victoria Station. You have been hit on the head.' The explanation was succinct and explanatory and was accompanied by a warm smile.

'I can feel it. Where… where is the other man? The one who hit me?'

She shrugged. 'I don't know. Would you like a cup of tea?'

'No, no. I must be going.'

'You'll be going nowhere.' This injunction came from a second figure who appeared beside the nurse. It was a police sergeant: a robust red-faced fellow with a comfortable girth.

'You've got a lot of explaining to do, my lad,' he said as though he was admonishing a youngster for breaking a window with his cricket ball.

'Horsefield – did he escape?'

'If you mean the bloke what dinted your skull; yes, he legged it.'

'He's a killer.'

'Is he now? And was it him that did for the bloke in the lavatories.'

Salter. I had forgotten about him. 'Oh, he's dead, then.'

'As a doornail.'

'The man that I was chasing, a fellow called Horsefield, was the dead man's accomplice in a bank robbery… I'm a private detective.'

The sergeant held up his hand. 'Whoa. Save your breath, son. You can tell it all to Inspector Sullivan. He's on his way here now.'

'In the meantime,' said the nurse, 'how about that cup of tea and a couple of aspirins.'

I nodded in acceptance and another hand grenade exploded in my skull.

The sergeant disappeared, but the nurse sat with me as I drank my tea. She told me her name was Ivana and she was Russian. She was originally from Stalingrad but had left the city at the outbreak of the war and made her way to England. Her family had perished in the terrible battle for the city in 1942 and now she was alone in the world. She seemed to gain some comfort telling me her story – a stranger whom she would never see again. A stranger whom she expected to be carted off to prison any moment now.

Her eyes misted as she spoke of her parents and the terrible atrocities that the Nazis had wrought in Stalingrad.

She had a strong face, mannish almost, but a lovely smile and deep expressive brown eyes.

I liked her.

Suddenly there was a rustle behind the screens and then Inspector Bernard Sullivan appeared.

'Oh, it's you,' he said.

* * *

Sullivan knew me from my days as a serving policeman. He was a copper of the old school: fair, scrupulous and down to earth.

'I'd heard you'd gone private. A ladies detective. Spying through keyholes on naughty husbands. So how come you get mixed up in a murder and a nasty affray in a railway station?'

'Just luck,' I said and he laughed.

'O.K. Johnny. Give me the low-down,' he said pulling up a stool.

As succinctly as I could I filled him in him on the scenario involving Malcolm Salter and Bruce Horsefield. Sullivan listened intently, his eyes twitching all the while, a sign I knew that he was making a mental note of all that I was telling him. He was that kind of copper.

After I'd finished, he rubbed his chin sagely. 'A bit of a mess all round. You O.K.?'

I touched my head where Horsefield's gun had landed and found to my surprise that it was bandaged. 'I'll live,' I said.

'A good night's kip and a stiff brandy, as my old granny used to say.'

'So Salter's dead.'

'The bloke in the lav. Yes. He hung on for a while but he didn't make it.'

'And the money.'

'Well Sergeant Morris found a bag but it was empty.

That'd be the one, I reckon.'

'Yes. It had two thousand pounds in it.'

Sullivan whistled. 'Nice little horde. So it looks like your mate Horsefield got away with it after all.'

'Yes,' I said disconsolately. 'It looks like it.'

Sullivan gave a wry chuckle. 'Not your finest hour, then; eh, Johnny? Perhaps you'd better get back to one of those keyholes, watching those naughty married people.'

'Ha ha,' I replied, for want of a wittier or more acerbic response. 'Does that mean I can go?'

'Well, I reckon so. We know where to pick up you up if needed. You say it's Herbert whose handling the Chelmsford robbery?'

'Yes.'

Sullivan beamed. 'Well, it will be my pleasure to dump this little lot in his lap. You may find him on your doorstep in the morning. The grin converted into a chuckle. He rose from the stool. Before he disappeared behind the screens he turned back and gave me a friendly nod. 'Look after yourself, lad,' he said.

TWENTY-TWO

Tired, disheartened and hungry, Peter dragged his weary bones towards the bus stop. It was time for him to return home. His search had been fruitless. His bright hopes had been dashed. Perhaps detective work wasn't as satisfying as he thought it would be. It was a little devil of a thought and he quelled it. You need perseverance and determination to succeed as a private investigator, he told himself firmly. You don't give up if at first you don't succeed. He knew this was true but it was hard to accept when his feet hurt and his tummy rumbled.

'Perseverance and determination,' he muttered, almost as a mantra. 'Perseverance and determination. And luck,' he added as an afterthought. Yes, luck was what he had lacked today. 'If only I'd had a bit of luck...'

And then he did. It came out of nowhere and pinned him to the spot. He froze like a statue as he observed a tall thin man turn the corner, walking in a slow awkward fashion towards him. Peter could not see his face clearly because it was shielded by a large grey felt hat.

His heart almost stopped at the excitement of this encounter. Surely, here was the man himself. The one that he'd been searching for. He rubbed his eyes to make sure this wasn't an hallucination. It wasn't. Here was Bruce Horsefield. In the flesh. He was sure of it. He stared at him as he walked past and noticed that there was a dark stain on one of his trouser legs below the knee – the leg that seemed to be giving him some discomfort.

The man was injured – that explained his rather clumsy gait.

Horsefield took no notice of Peter as he slipped past him,

making slow but steady progress along the pavement. Peter waited only a few seconds before turning and following the man.

After some ten minutes when Horsefield had led Peter into the maze of small streets lying behind Middlesex Road, he reached a row of down at heel terrace houses. Here Horsefield paused and gazed around him as though he was checking he hadn't been followed. Peter had the presence of mind to push his body into the tangle of an overgrown privet hedge, some of the prickly branches getting up his nose.

Believing himself safe from shadows, Horsefield mounted the steps of one house and disappeared inside.

Peter gazed at the gaunt shabby building, its mildewed façade and blank windows, darkened by the blackout shutters which were still in place, and smiled. The villain's hideout, he thought. He had found it. All on his own.

He must inform Johnny and how proud he would be in doing so. He remembered passing a telephone box a few streets away and sprinting he retraced his way there. Frustratingly, it was occupied by a young woman with a brightly coloured turban and large dangly earrings. She was in full flow. He could hear her voice in high-pitched moaning mode as her left hand fluttered wildly like a trapped bat. He couldn't catch her words but one didn't have to in order to know she was expressing some grievance in a grumpy tirade.

'Come on, come on,' murmured Peter in frustration, glancing at his watch. He was well aware that it was quite possible that Horsefield would only stay in the house a short time before moving on. The woman in the box sensing his presence and his impatience glowered at him and then turned her back without a pause in her diatribe.

Seconds ticked by into minutes. Then to his great dismay,

he saw the woman put more coins into the slot. God, she was going to tell all the world about her grievance.

Peter was joined by a tall smartly dressed man outside the box. A queue was forming.

'Has she been in long?' he asked.

'Forever,' said Peter.

The man leaned forward and tapped on the glass of the telephone box. The woman turned abruptly, scowled and mouthed some obscenity at him.

'Charming,' he said.

At last, the woman put the phone down, but made no real effort to leave the box.

The man pulled the door open. 'Have you done?'

'Yeah, yeah,' she returned scowling. 'This is private in here. You should wait.'

'I have been waiting. I have an important call to make.'

With a belligerent shove, she brushed past him. 'It's all yours,' she said.

The man turned to Peter. 'It is rather important, sonny. I hope you don't mind if I go before you.'

Peter's nerves along with his temper were somewhat frayed by now and he wasn't going to have this. He had waited his turn and his turn it was.

'Yes, I bloody do mind,' he found himself saying, swearing out loud in front of a grown up for the first time in his life. Without waiting for a reaction, he yanked the door from the man's grasp and entered the box.

As his nervous fingers pressed the coins into the slot, he prayed that Johnny would be in his office. It was teatime. Surely, whatever he'd been dong all day, he'd be back for a cuppa and his usual makeshift evening meal.

But the phone kept on ringing.

In his mind's eye, Peter saw the lonely instrument on Johnny's desk, the dim shadows of evening falling softly onto it as it vibrated gently in the gloom, but there was no arm there to reach out and pick up the receiver. Eventually, he gave up and pressed button B.

With a sigh, he dialled another number. This time the call was answered.

'Hello,' said a voice in a tone that intimated that the caller had interrupted something of vital importance.

'Benny. It's Peter.'

'Oh, Peter, hello, my boy. What a pleasure to hear from you.' The voice was sweeter, friendlier now, rich in warmth.

'Benny, is Johnny there at the café?'

'Not unless he's the invisible man. He doesn't come here as often as he used to... not since...' The voice trailed away.

'Do you know where he is?'

'How should I? Trailing some hoodlum maybe or taking a drink at the Velvet Cage. Your guess is as good as mine.'

Peter ruffled his hair with his free hand. 'Look, Benny, it's important I get a message to him. It's about his latest case.'

'What message?'

'I've tracked Horsefield to his lair. It's 23 Commercial Street, Houndsditch.'

'Let me write this down. Hey, wait a minute, what do you mean you tracked this horseperson to his lair. Are you in danger? What's going on?'

'No, no, I'm safe but I don't know how long Horsefield will stay there. Johnny needs to get here fast.'

'Are you sure you're safe? You shouldn't be involving yourself in such activities.'

'I'm fine, Benny; don't worry about me.'

'Of course I worry. No more funerals do I want to go to this year.'

'Look this is urgent. Please try and get in touch with Johnny. I've rung his office but he's not there. Maybe you could try the Velvet Cage.'

'Very well.'

'Oh, and could you ring Aunt Edith and Aunt Martha with some excuse of why I won't be home for tea. I don't want them to worry.'

'A web of lies.'

'Just a little fib. I'd better go I don't want to leave Horsefield for too long.'

'Be careful, my boy. Be very careful.'

Peter replaced the receiver quickly and exited the phone box. The man waiting outside glared at him, but Peter had other things on his mind and did not notice. Breaking into a sprint, he headed back to 23 Commercial Street.

TWENTY-THREE

Even before Frances Sexton entered his house, he knew that there was something wrong. It was instinct rather than evidence at first. As he walked up the path, he experienced a strange, irrational sensation as though a shadow had fallen over him and he shivered. When he discovered the front door was unlocked, it was no longer instinct. His heart constricted and a desperate inner panic took hold of him. Flinging down his case in the hall he raced to the cellar, his terror growing with every step. Before he got there, he knew what he would find – the unlocked front door had told him that much. Nevertheless, when he entered the gloomy chamber and saw the empty bed, and the blood-smeared handcuff, his legs grew weak and his body shook with horror. Within seconds of entering the cellar, he found himself leaning against the wall while his stomach retched, attempting to propel his midday meal on to the floor. With Herculean effort, Sexton controlled this powerful reaction, groaning with despair as he did so.

The repercussions of this nightmare situation that the empty room presented were so frightening and impenetrable that at first Sexton's mind could not cope with them. He just slithered to the floor and placed his head in his hands and groaned again, while rocking to and fro on his haunches.

Northcote had escaped. Northcote was free. Now Northcote could destroy him.

And he had no idea what to do.

He sat there for some fifteen minutes or so, his mind fixated on that one and only fact: Northcote had escaped. The bastard was free!

Eventually, he dragged himself to his feet and, like a sleep-walker, made his way back upstairs and to the drinks cabinet where he poured himself an enormous brandy.

He took a large gulp before slumping down in an armchair, clasping the glass tightly between his two hands.

He had no idea what he was going to do – or what he could do. His tired, ragged brain revealed to him that there were no options. He certainly couldn't go to the police. He had no idea what Northcote would do next or where he would go and so there was no hope of recapturing him. And, of course, his dream of using him as a scapegoat was in tatters.

Or was it?

Oh, God, he didn't know. He just couldn't think straight.

More brandy might help. He reached out for the bottle.

* * *

In the shady environs of Cartwright Gardens, Dr Ralph Northcote waited for the dark. He had found himself cheap lodgings in the King's Cross area and was now ready – more than ready after years of incarceration – to kill. There would be an extra frisson to the act tonight, not just because it would be the first time in years, although this fact was mightily significant to him, but also because he would fatally wound that traitorous swine, Sexton. Sitting on a bench in the shadow of a large plane tree, he watched the moon as it grew brighter while the blue of the evening sky deepened. Soon it was an eerily yellow orb hanging against an indigo setting. A hunter's moon and he was a very eager hunter indeed.

* * *

There was one stretch of the Caledonian Road, about half a mile from King's Cross Station, that to Sally Hopkins's mind was darker than the rest. She knew that the blackout was the blackout, but somehow this section seemed to have an added layer of inky darkness. There was a line of tall, blank featureless commercial buildings which towered above the road, standing like grim sentries which seemed to her vivid imagination, as though they were waiting to pounce on an unsuspecting pedestrian. Every night when she walked home after her stint as a barmaid in one of the public houses up by the station, her pace quickened when she reached this part of her route. She knew she was being illogical, but she couldn't help her feelings. And tonight strangely she felt more frightened than usual.

She had good reason.

Suddenly a dark shape stepped out in front of her, causing her to collide with it. Sally Hopkins gave out a little scream but her attention was immediately taken by the sudden pain in her abdomen. She pulled away from the figure, the pain increasing, but the man – she now recognised the shape as a man – came towards her again and thrust something towards her stomach. She moaned with pain and sank to the floor. Feeling dizzy and faint, she gazed up at her assailant and saw that he was holding what appeared to be a knife. As consciousness faded, she became aware of the wetness that was seeping through the material of her coat.

Blood.

The man knelt down beside her and without a word, stabbed her again, this time twisting the knife in the wound. She hadn't the energy to cry out. Her mouth opened, spittle dripped down her chin and then her head fell back on the pavement.

Within seconds Sally Hopkins was dead.

With a satisfied murmur, Ralph Northcote dragged the body down a narrow opening between two buildings, to a small area hidden from the road where the dustbins were kept. Here, he lit a candle, placed it on one of the dustbin lids and then undressed the girl. In the pale shimmering light, he extracted the instruments he needed from the bag he had left there and began work.

* * *

Half an hour later, he had completed his task, having removed the heart, liver and a section of the left thigh and wrapped them in newspaper before stowing them in his case. For a moment he gazed down at the girl's face, now gently laced with blood, the eyes and mouth still wide with shock and horror. He felt nothing for her. No emotion touched his heart or mind. She was just dead meat to him.

He was ready to go, but he still had one task to perform. Taking Francis Sexton's silver cigarette case from his pocket, he placed it on the ground near the body. This action did prompt a reaction: a gentle, unstable giggle.

TWENTY-FOUR

When Inspector Bernard Sullivan had departed, I intended to do the same. I reckoned I needed a drink and some thinking time. And, boy, did I have something to think about. However, when I swung my legs around on the camp bed and attempted to stand up, the room began to bend and sway. With a groan, I slumped back staring at the ceiling waiting for it to settle down. Then into my field of vision appeared the face of nurse Ivana.

'You are a naughty man,' she said in her rich Russian voice, making it sound like an invitation to an orgy. 'You cannot move just yet. You must rest for a couple of hours at least. Your system has had a very big shock. You lie back. I will bring you a cup of sweet tea.'

'You couldn't make that a double whisky, could you?' I grinned, in spite of my discomfort.

She returned my smile. 'You really are a naughty man.'

'No ice,' I added with a chuckle as she disappeared around the screen. She returned a few minutes later with a mug of hot, sweet tea.

'Just as you ordered: no ice,' she beamed, as she handed it to me. 'Now drink that and rest for a while.'

'Yes, ma'am.'

The tea was good despite the sweetness and I did feel as though it revived me a little, but I still hadn't the energy or the sureness of foot to get up and leave and so I obeyed nurse's orders and lay back and stared at the gently shimmering ceiling. In the distance I could hear station noises, the echoing hiss of steam, speaker announcements, the shrill screech of a guard's whistle and the muted cacophony of the sea of travellers as they ebbed and flowed up and down the concourse and the various platforms. So many lives, so many journeys. It seemed that despite the drama I was involved in, the world was getting on with its mundane business.

I closed my eyes and ran through the events of the day. It struck me that I'd been lucky. I could be lying on a slab in the morgue now instead of a fairly comfy camp bed being nursed by a very pleasant Russian girl. The mystery surrounding Annie Salter's death had been cleared up once and for all, but unfortunately the real villain of the piece, her murderer, had escaped. Strangely I felt sorry for Malcolm Salter. I knew he had been a deserter and an armed robber, (past tense) but I didn't think he deserved to die in such a manner. Some leopards can change their spots and I'm a strong believer in giving a chap a chance at reforming himself. Well, there was no chance for Malcolm now.

I suppose my part in the case was effectively over. I had carried out Father Sanderson's wishes and discovered the truth of poor old Annie's death. However, I knew I couldn't let it rest there. I had to find Horsefield and bring him to justice. If only in revenge for the gargantuan headache he'd given me. And besides, surely it is what the old priest would have expected me to do. Well, I was going to do it. Or at least try.

Mind you, I had no idea how I was going to do it. I reckoned that I would have a go at formulating some sort of plan after a good night's sleep when I hoped the blitzkrieg in my head had ceased.

I gave a shrug, closed my eyes and, before I knew it, I had fallen into a gentle sleep.

I was woken sometime later by my Russian nightingale. She had her raincoat on and seemed to be ready to go somewhere.

'I've just come to say goodbye,' she said with a smile. 'My shift is over and Nurse Kerry is taking over.'

I glanced at my watch. It was just after six in the evening: I had been asleep for over three hours.

'You can stay here until you feel fit enough to leave.'

'Oh, that's now,' I said, pulling myself up more quickly than I should. My head throbbed as though a small road drill were digging deep into the convolutions of cerebral cortex but my vision, though not perfect, was much better. Everything seemed to have a fine double edge.

Ivana caught my arm. 'Whoa,' she said, with a half smile. 'Are you sure you're ready for this?'

Certainly am,' I said with more confidence than I felt, as I pulled myself to my feet. Thankfully the room stayed where it was, but the drills were still pounding away. 'Perhaps you could walk with me a while, just until I get my sea legs, as it were.'

Nurse Kerry, whose rosy red features had been peering around the screen, gave me an old-fashioned look.

'I suppose so,' said Ivana.

Breathing deeply, I stepped forward and took her arm. I needed it for my legs were still weak and unsure of themselves. We left the first aid room with me clinging to Ivana like some over attentive boyfriend. She seemed to take this strange perambulation in her own confident stride. Once outside the confines of the station, I began to breathe in the cool night air. It filled my lungs and began to clear away the cobwebs in my brain. Like some magic rejuvenating elixir, it coursed through my body giving me strength. After we had gone a hundred yards or so, I was walking normally again and my vision was clear, but I was reluctant to release my grip on Ivana's arm. It was good to be close to a woman again.

'I don't suppose you'd allow me to buy you a drink?' I

said as casually as I could.

'Now why do you suppose that? I'd love a drink.'

I grinned back sheepishly. 'I know just the place.'

* * *

It was around seven o'clock by the time we arrived at The Velvet Cage, my favourite watering hole. We had walked part of the way and then taken a taxi. It was quiet in the club, with very few customers and the musicians were only just setting up for their first set that evening.

We sat in a booth. Ivana asked for a sweet sherry – I grimaced at this but ordered the drink all the same while I settled for a whisky. For some time we sat in awkward silence. We seemed to have run out of conversation. We had chatted merrily on our journey, she telling me that she shared a small flat in Earl's Court with another nurse called Mildred and how she liked to read in her spare time 'the great British writers like Charles Dickens and Emily Bronte.' I had told her about my accident when I lost an eye and why I was a detective. 'So you get beaten up a lot,' she had observed wryly.

'I try not to be,' I said.

But now we seemed to have run out of steam. My supply of small talk was very limited at the best of times but now it seemed as though it had disappeared altogether.

Suddenly she turned to me and placed her hand on mine. 'You seem sad. I know you joke and smile, but I think you are a sad man. Why is that?'

I gave a non-committal smile.

'You perhaps have lost someone?'

'In this war, hasn't everyone? You, your parents.'

'Yes, that's true. But I hide my pain. I see yours in your face.'

'Look lady, I've just been bopped very hard on the head. No wonder you see pain in my face. Ouch!'

She grinned. 'Yes, you cover it up with a joke. Let me see your hands – your right hand.'

I held it up and wiggled my fingers. She took it gently and laid it palm upwards on the table and stared intently at it.

'Well,' she said, 'you will be pleased to know that you have a very healthy life line. You should live into an old age.'

Goodness, you're not going to read my palm?'

'Of course. All my family have the gift. The God-given lines on your hands tell many secrets about your character and your life. See, your heart line is strong and straight.'

'What does that mean?'

'You are idealistic and sometimes you let your heart rule your head.'

I took a drink of whisky. Can't argue with that, I thought, but said nothing.

'You are complex man, Johnny. Some of your lines do the oddest things.'

'Do they tell you whether I'm going to capture the fellow who tried to break my skull?'

She smiled and shook her head. 'I'm afraid not.'

I was about to make some flippant remark when I was conscious of a shadow falling over us and the heavy wheezing breathing of its owner.

I looked up and saw Benny, his face shiny with sweat and his eyes bulging from the exertions he had obviously just undergone. He mopped his brow with a handkerchief before he spoke. 'Johnny, thank heavens I've found you.'

'What is it, Benny? You look done in.'

'That's because I am. I ran most of the way. I'm so relieved you're here. Peter said you might be.'

'Peter? What about him?'

Benny shook his head. 'Such a foolish boy. Apparently,

he's been trailing one of your villains – the bank robber.'

'Horsefield!'

Benny nodded. 'I think that was his name. Well, Peter's traced him to an address in Houndsditch'. He paused to drag a scrap of paper from his pocket. '23 Commercial Street. He said he'd wait for you there, somewhere outside in the street.'

'The idiot. How long ago was this?'

'About twenty minute… half an hour ago.'

I turned abruptly to Ivana. 'I'm sorry, I have to go.'

'Of course.' She squeezed my hand. 'Be careful.'

'I'll try,' I said giving her a quick kiss on the cheek.

Without another word, I left the two of them staring after me as I dashed for the exit.

* * *

After a rather hectic and bumpy taxi ride, I arrived in Houndsditch. I asked the cabbie to drop me a few blocks away from Commercial Street. On the journey my mind had been trying to work out how Peter had ended up trailing Horsefield. He'd studied those bloody newspaper reports he'd shown me, hadn't he? No doubt on a hunch he'd gone down to Houndsditch and somehow by some fluke found where the fellow was hiding. I doubted if he realised how dangerous Horsefield was – especially now he was wounded and had managed to retrieve the cash from the bank robbery.

I suppose it was my fault that Peter fancied himself as a super sleuth, trying to impress me, and if he got hurt or worse, it would be on my conscience for life and possibly longer.

It was now quite dark as I turned into Commercial Street. The place was quiet and empty. There were no pedestrians and no traffic. An eerie silence seemed to inhabit the place. Casually, I lit a cigarette and strolled along the pavement noting the house numbers as I did so. Eventually I came to number 23. It was cloaked in total darkness which, of course, was not unusual in these days of the blackout. I looked around for Peter. There was no sign of the scamp.

Where the hell was he? What was he up to now? I called out his name, hoping that he would emerge from the shadows and greet me. But he didn't.

My heart sank.

What was I going to do now?

TWENTY-FIVE

David Llewellyn was cleaning his teeth prior to donning his pyjamas for an early night when the telephone rang.

'You'd better get that,' his wife Sylvia called from the bedroom. 'It's bound to be for you.'

She was right of course. He knew as he lifted the receiver that he could wave goodbye to the early appointment with his pillow.

'Sunderland, here, sir,' announced the tinny voice at the other end. 'There's been another murder. A young woman. Cut about something shocking. Looks like it's Northcote's work all right. She was found on Copenhagen Street, just off the Caledonian Road down by King's Cross. One of the local tarts stumbled over the body.'

Llewellyn gave a little groan as he felt the chill hand of fear grip him. It was happening all over again. The same nightmare, but this time somehow it was worse. The killer had turned into a phantom of the night. He had no idea where he was or where and when he would strike next.

'Give me the exact details and I'll be down there within the hour,' he said sourly.

* * *

The remains of Sally Hopkins were covered with a large grey blanket and part of the road had been cordoned off. Llewellyn stepped forward and raised the blanket, allowing the thin beam of his torch travel over the grisly corpse.

'Very nasty, eh, sir?' said Sunderland, standing close to him.

Llewellyn grunted a reply. 'Do we know what's been taken? The organs?'

'The pathologist says that her heart and liver have gone

and part of the thigh. He says he'll have a better idea when he examines the body back at the Yard.'

Llewellyn dropped the blanket. 'Well, get her back there, then. There's little use her being here.'

'Right, sir.'

Llewellyn was about to turn away when something caught his attention. The beam of his torch fell on something that glittered in the gloom at the far side of the blanket, in the shadows over by the wall. He stepped forward, bent down and picked it up. Holding it close to his face, he saw that it was a silver cigarette case.'

'Very interesting,' he said slowly, his eyes widening with surprise.

'Do you think it was dropped by the killer, sir?' asked Sunderland.

'I'm not sure, but what makes it interesting – fascinating even – is that it has a name engraved on it.'

'Not Northcote?'

'No. Not Northcote. The name is Francis Sexton.'

* * *

While Inspector David Llewellyn was examining the cigarette case of Dr Francis Sexton, the man himself was preparing for his great vanishing act. After wallowing sometime in despair, following the discovery that his prisoner Northcote had escaped, the section in his brain that dealt with self preservation and survival had suddenly kicked in. He realised that his only course of action now was to disappear. Go somewhere in the country – maybe Devon where he had spent many childhood holidays. He had to become someone else in an out-of-the-way place, where neither the authorities nor Northcote could find him. With this vague and desperate plan in mind, he was quickly packing a bag with essentials, including a few small valuable items which he could sell to help him get by, along with the fifty pounds he had taken from his wall safe.

With a great strength of will, he was not allowing his mind to dwell on his old life which he now had to leave behind. If he was to survive – and indeed it was a matter of survival – he realised that he must forget all that and accept the new and unpleasant, drastic circumstances in which he found himself.

Clutching his case, he headed for the hallway and retrieved his hat and coat. Once he had donned these, he couldn't resist stepping back into the living room to cast a final eye over his home.

It was then that it struck him. He just couldn't depart like this. Walk out and leave all this behind intact. It wasn't just the fact that he was turning his back on the comfort and security of his home but, in a more practical sense, he couldn't leave the house like the Marie Celeste, like a ghost home, still keeping the signs of recent habitation: discarded newspapers, crumpled sheets, half empty gin bottles. And more importantly he couldn't leave the cellar: the room where Northcote had been kept prisoner for prying eyes and expert analysts. That would really give the game away. That canny Welsh policeman would very quickly put two and two together and make a sparkling four.

Although he was aware that he was tired, his brain frayed at the edges and his thinking processes ragged and shaky, he also knew that the idea that came to him now was the right one.

He would torch the house.

Burn it to the ground.

The flames would expunge, purge any evidence useful to the police. With a smile he realised that the added bonus of this idea would be that they might think that he had perished in the flames. It would be a sound assumption to make. Then he really would be off the hook. They might search for a body, but he knew that the war had taught the police to cut corners. There were too many burnt out buildings and missing corpses to cope with efficiently. Whatever, setting fire to the place would certainly buy him time.

Inspired by this notion, he dropped his case and headed outside to the garage where he kept a spare can of petrol. That would ensure the flames would be all-devouring.

He chuckled to himself as he unlocked the garage door and swung it open. So focussed was he in his task, that he failed to see a bulky shadow by the gate. Dragging a metal canister from a shelf at the rear of the garage, Sexton returned to the house, followed at a distance by the shadow.

Once back inside the house, Sexton went down into the cellar, unscrewed the top of the canister and began sloshing the petrol around in a liberal fashion before returning to the sitting room. Here he repeated the process, dousing the carpet, the sofa and the curtains. He smiled broadly. He felt there was something satisfying about being an agent of destruction.

Soon the canister was empty and he flung it down and then stood for a moment breathing in the fumes. The aroma was intoxicating and pleasing. Then he heard a slight movement behind him and turning swiftly he saw a figure standing in the doorway. His heart juddered with shock.

It was Ralph Northcote.

'Trying to destroy the evidence?' he said quietly.

The sight of Northcote immediately ignited Sexton's anger. He gave no thought as to how or why the devil came to be standing in his sitting room. Rage exploded within him. He roared with fury and like an automaton moved stiffly towards him, his arms outstretched.

Northcote stayed put. He simply lifted his right arm

which held a long sharp knife.

'Stay,' he snapped, as one would to a dog. 'Stay, or I will gouge your eyes out.'

Sexton faltered and then did as he was told.

'I know it is melodramatic,' Northcote said quietly, without any emotion, 'but I have returned for my revenge.' He gazed about him. 'And it seems as though you have helped me in my preparations.'

Sexton took a step forward, but Northcote thrust the knife towards him. 'It would be foolish to come any closer. I cannot tell you how much pleasure it would be for me to cut you up, to hear you cry in agony – the man that tried to deceive me. The man that imprisoned me and treated me like an animal.'

Sexton's mind sought in vain for some course of action. He knew he could not reason with Northcote. He knew he could not tackle him: one false move and he would feel the blade of that vicious knife on his face. Could he perhaps run? But where to? Northcote was blocking the only viable exit to the outside. If he turned and ran into the kitchen, he knew that the exterior door was locked. By the time he had retrieved the key, the fiend would be upon him. The situation seemed hopeless.

'Not only will you die tonight,' Northcote was saying, 'but your secret will be exposed. The police will know all about you.'

Sexton shook his head. He didn't know what the fellow was talking about and besides he was only half listening while his eyes darted around the room in search of something he could snatch up and use as a weapon against Northcote. His eyes lit upon a large glass ashtray on the coffee table to his left, just a few feet beyond his reach. He knew he would have to risk it. It was his only chance.

Slowly he stepped backwards and then in a desperate

sideways motion he reached out for the ashtray, but Northcote had sensed what was happening and attacked. He lunged forward thrusting the knife at Sexton, who had moved so quickly that the blade only caught him in the arm. With a cry of pain, Sexton stumbled sideways on to the edge of the sofa, where he lost his balance and crashed to the floor.

Northcote stood over him, legs astride like a maniacal colossus and raised the knife, ready for the fatal blow. In wild desperation, Sexton lashed out with his legs, catching Northcote violently in the crotch. With a moan, Northcote doubled up, the knife spinning from his hand. Scrabbling across the floor from his assailant, Sexton reached out for the ashtray once more and brought it crashing down on Northcote's head. With a muted grunt, Northcote slithered forward onto his face in an apparent faint.

The light of unstable triumph illuminated Sexton's eyes as he rose unsteadily to his feet and stood panting over the inert frame of his enemy, the throbbing pain in his shoulder almost forgotten. He was inclined to bring the ashtray down once more on the man's skull, but he resisted the temptation. The flames would finish the job off more satisfactorily.

He felt in his jacket pocket for his cigarette lighter, wincing as he did so, the pain of his wounded arm reasserting itself. Taking an old newspaper from the magazine rack, he twisted it round into a makeshift torch and lit one end with the lighter. It blossomed into a bright yellow flame. With a satisfied grin, he flung the burning paper onto the petrol soaked hearth rug. It spluttered awhile and for a moment Sexton thought that it would go out, but then with a gentle woomf, tendrils of flame shot across the rug and rose upwards. Within seconds, the hungry fire, with the help of the petrol, reached out beyond the rug to touch the carpet and other items of furniture with its fiery contagion.

Sexton was surprised and pleased at the speed with which the fire was spreading. Already he could feel the searing heat on his face and he knew that he had little time to lose before he left the building. But as he turned to go, he stumbled. Something had caught hold of his ankle.

Someone.

Northcote.

The fiend had roused himself. Sexton tried to wrench himself free of his firm grip but failed. He dropped to the floor, kicking his leg as violently as he could in an attempt to shake his assailant off. All the while the flames were multiplying, growing hungrier and more fierce.

'Let go, or we'll both be killed,' screamed Sexton.

Surprisingly Northcote released his hold, while at the same time, jumping to his feet and scooping up the knife which lay inches away from the devouring flames. Sexton could only see him now as a dark silhouette against the yellow wall of fire.

For a second time Northcote loured over him but Sexton was too slow to react on this occasion. With a snarl of anger, Northcote brought the knife down, straight into Sexton's right eye and piercing his brain. Sexton opened his mouth to cry out but no sound emerged. His body jiggled for a few seconds like a man on a gibbet and then lay still, a trickle of blood smearing his cheek.

Fixing that pleasing image in his mind, Northcote ran from the burning building out into the enveloping darkness.

TWENTY-SIX

I made my way up the overgrown path of number 23 Commercial Street. It seemed to me that the house had not been occupied for some time. The door was boarded up as were the downstairs windows. However, on closer inspection, I noticed that one of the boards across the window at the left-hand side of the door seemed to be hanging loose. So it proved to be. With just a gentle movement I was able to swing the board to one side, creating a gap big enough for me to gain entry to the house, a feat managed easily as the window pane behind the planking was missing. It lay in shattered shards on the floor inside.

In a trice I was standing in a dark, damp and rank smelling chamber. I lit a match and the decaying room sprang into flickering relief. This had been the sitting room, I guessed, noting the broken down horsehair sofa and a decrepit armchair, the seat of which seemed now to be the home for a family of mice. As the match dimmed, prior to going out, I heard a movement somewhere in the room and then as darkness returned, a bright light shone in my face.

'Johnny!' a voice called. It was Peter. I felt a mixture of relief and annoyance.

'Take that torch out of my eyes, will you?' I snapped.

'Sorry,' he said, lowering the beam.

'What the hell are you doing here?'

'I followed Horsefield. I saw him enter the house but now he's disappeared.'

'What do you mean disappeared?'

'I watched him climb through the gap in the boarded up window and come in here just before it got dark but he didn't come out again, so I came in after him.'

'You little fool, don't you know the man is very dangerous? He's a murderer. He wouldn't think twice of putting a bullet in you.'

'I was careful.'

I rolled my eyes in angry derision but, of course, in the darkness Peter could not see disdain.

'Anyway, I've been around the house and looked in all the rooms and he's not here,' he continued. 'He must have left another way, probably out of the back.'

'Are you sure he's gone?'

'Positive.'

'That's very odd. What made him come here in the first place if it wasn't to hide out.'

'He might come back.'

'I suppose so, but I reckon that's unlikely. When you saw him was he limping?'

'Yes. His left leg, I think.'

'That's my handiwork. I wounded the fellow today.'

'Really!' In his excitement at this revelation, Peter's voice rose an octave. 'How?'

As briefly and succinctly as I could, I gave Peter a recital of my adventures at Victoria Station.'

'Wow, a real shoot out. That's terrific.'

'Not all that terrific. The man got away and with the money after killing his greedy partner and giving me a whopping headache.'

'So, what's our plan of action?'

A good question. I pushed my hat back on my head and scratched my forehead. I was puzzled and no ideas were coming to my rescue.

'Well,' I said at length. 'There's nothing we can do here tonight. Let's get you home.'

'Ah, Johnny, we can't give up now.'

'Oh, yes we can, partner. We have no leads and even if I had, I certainly wouldn't be involving you in following them up.'

'Why not? I found Horsefield, didn't I?'

I couldn't argue with that point. Then an idea struck me. 'When you saw Horsefield, was he carrying a bag, like a small holdall?'

Peter thought for a moment. 'Yes, I reckon he was. He sort of clutched something to his chest as if he was holding a baby. I suppose it could have been a holdall.'

I grinned. 'Holding a baby, eh? His bonny baby: two thousand smackeroos in crisp bank notes. So that's why he came here.'

Peter shook his head in puzzlement. 'What do you mean?'

'To stash away the money. A nice little hiding place while the heat is on. This is his neck of the woods. He'd know about this old house. An ideal location to secrete the stolen cash. Safe as old houses.'

'So it's here somewhere,'

'Somewhere. Yes, I reckon it is.'

'So we'd better search for it.' Peter was getting really excited now.

'Whoa,' I cried. 'You've heard the phrase 'needle in a haystack', well that's the situation we have here. Old house full of various nooks and crannies. Pitch black and a small torch. How on earth are we going to be able to search for a small bag containing some stolen loot?'

Peter gave a heavy sigh. 'I see what you mean.'

'I need to contact Inspector Sullivan about this – get him to send a body of men to keep an eye on the house and when it's daylight give it a thorough search.'

'And what about Horsefield? Where do you think he'll be now? What if he comes back tonight?'

'I don't think he'll do that. He needs to rest up… to…' My

mouth stopped working mid-sentence as my brain took over and an idea formed slowly in my mind.

'What is it, Johnny?' Peter asked after a brief pause.

'He'll need medical treatment – for his leg. The wound needs cleaning and bandaging. He can't go to a hospital. They'd ask too many questions. So would a doctor. Where would he go for help and a bit of simple nursing?'

'His mother. He'd go to his mother.'

'Indeed, he would. She lives in the neighbourhood.'

'I went there this morning. To her house.'

'What!'

'I pretended I wanted a glass of water. I tried to spy out to see if Horsefield was there – but I got nowhere. She gave me the glass of water but I didn't get past the front door.'

'Well our man certainly wasn't there this morning – he had other fish to fry then… at Victoria Station – but I reckon there's a strong chance that he'll be there now.'

'Ok, let's go.'

'Not on your life, Peter. I'm not risking taking you with me. As I've told you Horsefield is a very dangerous man. Even more so now that he's got his loot.'

'Oh, come on, Johnny. Look, I can help you, I know. All we need to do is establish that Horsefield is at his mother's and then we can call in the police.' He reached out his hand squeezed my arm. 'Come on, Johnny, we can do that together, can't we?'

TWENTY-SEVEN

In the distance David Llewellyn could see a bright crimson smear illuminating the sky as they turned down the road where Francis Sexton lived.

'There's been no bombing tonight, has there, sir?' asked Sergeant Sunderland as he manoeuvred the car slowly towards the fiery glow.

'No,' David replied slowly, as he peered ahead of him and caught sight of a fire engine and the darting silhouettes of firemen. 'But it looks like our suspect's house is blazing away nicely.'

Sunderland parked the car some hundred yards from the conflagration and the two men walked slowly towards the burning house. Even from this distance, they could feel the heat of the conflagration blowing towards them in waves. However, the flames were beginning to surrender to the force of the water and a mixture of steam and smoke were beginning to envelope the damaged building like a surreal bank of fog. Llewellyn made his way through a small knot of onlookers and approached one of the firemen who seemed to be in charge.

'What's happened here?' he asked.

The man turned abruptly, his sweaty face tinged red from the reflection of the flames.' Stand well back, sir. It's not safe for you.'

'I'm a police officer,' said Llewellyn drawing out his warrant card. 'I need to know.'

'Oh,' responded the fireman, a little nonplussed. 'Well, I can't tell you much. A neighbour called us when she saw the flames. We think there's a body in there but we couldn't reach it. The heat was too intense by the time we arrived.

We've got it under control now, but there won't be much left of the house when it's over. Now if you'll excuse me.' He moved forward and began issuing orders to a group of men wielding one of the hoses.

Llewellyn passed a knowing glance at his colleague. 'This is a funny business. If there is a body in there, I'd like to know whose it is.'

'Well, if it's Sexton, that saves us a lot of work.'

'Indeed. That might be too convenient though.' He gave a harsh laugh. 'Still, I'm a cynical old bastard.'

Slapping Sunderland on the back, he turned to go. 'Come on. We can't do anything here for the moment. I have an appointment with a pillow.'

The two men began walking back to the car. They were oblivious of a tall, bulky man standing amid the throng of onlookers who studied their every movement.

It was Dr Ralph Northcote, who had stayed behind to watch the resulting finale of his handiwork. He had been shocked to see Llewellyn turn up on the scene. David Llewellyn, the man responsible for his foul years of imprisonment in Newfield House. He had forgotten about him. Something in his psyche had blanked this cursed policeman from his consciousness. He had not thought of Llewellyn for years. But now, seeing him again, suddenly all his anger and hatred for the man welled up inside him once more. If ever anyone in his life deserved to die, Llewellyn did. He had been the one that had done for him. Had exposed him. Had consigned him to a life of ignominy and imprisonment.

Northcote had to control himself from rushing forward then and there and grabbing the bastard by the neck, throttling the life out of him. He could feel his fingers sink into the soft flesh of the policeman's throat. He saw the eyes bulge in terror as he tightened his grip. He could hear that strange thin reedy death whistle as Llewellyn's lungs gave up the ghost. He felt the body slump against him, the dead mouth damp with spittle…

But Northcote didn't move. Some instinct of self-preservation stopped him. It can wait, a voice told him. *He* can wait. The anticipation would add further pleasure to the deed. But Northcote knew that the death of David Llewellyn was to be his next project.

* * *

Northcote waited until the two policemen had returned to their car and driven away before he moved. Giving one more glance to the glowing ruins of Sexton's house, he turned and walked with slow deliberation back down the road, away from the blaze that he had started, the furnace in which lay the blackened remains of the man whom he had thought was his saviour but who turned out to be his cruellest enemy. Now he just regretted that he didn't have the time and opportunity to take a piece of Sexton's flesh as a tasty souvenir. But this was not a time for regrets or for dwelling on the past. He was free – the shackles of Newfield House and Sexton's cellar had been severed. He really was free now – and he had a new passion to make his pulses race. The destruction of Detective Inspector David Llewellyn.

* * *

Sheila Llewellyn heard her husband climb the stairs and sigh heavily as he reached the landing. She glanced at the phosphorescent numbers on the alarm clock on her tiny bedside table. It was nearly three in the morning. David's shadowy figure appeared in the bedroom.

'Are you all right?' she murmured.

'I'm fine,' came the weary unconvincing response from the darkness.

'Do you want a cup of tea or anything?'

'No, love. You don't disturb yourself. Get back to sleep.'

'Aren't you coming to bed?'

'In a while. I need to calm down a bit.'

'Bad night?'

He did not reply but bent over the bed and gave her a kiss on the cheek. 'Nothing for you to worry about, love. You get your beauty sleep.'

Sheila knew it was David's way. When he was really depressed about a case, he would keep it all to himself. He would not bother her with his troubles. It was part of his chivalrous nature. She had learned to live with it. Matters would not be improved if she started to probe. From very early on in their relationship she had realised that he compartmentalised his police work, never letting the detail of it spill over into his private life. It was his way of protecting her from the darkness in his life.

'If you're sure,' she murmured sleepily.

He kissed her again. 'I'm sure, my lovely.'

'O.K.' Within minutes Sheila Llewellyn was fast asleep again, while her husband sat in his favourite armchair downstairs, with only a small table lamp for illumination, puffing discontentedly on a series of cigarettes.

TWENTY-EIGHT

Peter and I stood in the shadows on the opposite side of the road from Bruce Horsefield's mother's house. Like all other dwellings in the road it seemed to be in total darkness. This was a result of the blackout curtains or shutters which not only deceived the Hun, but a weary private detective and his eager young assistant also. The problem was how to ascertain whether Horsefield was inside the building, resting his wounded leg and receiving succour from his mother without alerting the occupants of the place – whoever they may be.

'I could go and listen by the front room window and at the kitchen round the back,' said Peter. 'I might be able to hear voices.'

'You might hear voices, but it's unlikely you'll hear what's being said and whether Horsefield is one of the speakers or not.'

Peter shrugged in response. 'Well, have you a better idea?' he said with an air of petulance.

He had me there. In truth, I really didn't want Peter with me. He was too young – and to be frank – too inexperienced to be involved in such a job. He was more likely to be an encumbrance than a help and I was concerned for his safety. But I was stuck with him.

'Let's make our way around to the back of the house and see if there is anyway of getting inside without being detected.

Peter's eyes lit up. 'Great,' he said.

To approach the rear of the building we had to make our way down a narrow track which cut between the row of houses three doors down. This gave us access to the lane that ran behind all the dwellings along that stretch.

Once we had reached the rear of the Horsefield dwelling, I pulled Peter to me and whispered harshly in his ear: 'You are to stay here on guard…' I held up my hand and placed it over his mouth before he could protest. 'No ifs or buts, my boy. This is important. Listen! I am going to try and gain entry and see if I can locate Mr Horsefield. You are to stay here and wait. If I am not out of there within fifteen minutes, you must go for the police. Do not, I repeat, do not attempt to come in after me. Do you understand?'

In the dim starlight, I could see the disappointed look on Peter's face deepen. He wanted adventure and excitement; standing guard outside did not quite fit in with his concept of thrilling detective work.

'Don't let me down. It's very important that you do as I ask. Understood?'

He gave me a reluctant mute nod.

I had to trust him – but I knew that he could be reckless and impulsive.

'Now hand over that little torch of yours. I reckon that'll be very useful.'

He did so without a word.

Good lad,' I said. 'Fifteen minutes,' I repeated, as I slipped over the garden wall and made my way to the back door.

With the small pencil torch, I examined the lock. It was old and rusty. And easily dealt with. Within a minute, I had manipulated the fragile workings with my nail file and gained entry. The beam of the torch informed me that I was in some kind of laundry room. The finger of feeble light picked out a large sink, a tub and posser, and a mangle, while a drying cradle laden with damp greying garments hung menacingly over my head like some giant surreal spider waiting to pounce. I stood in the darkness and listened. A muffled sound from some far room came to my ears. It sounded like a radio playing.

Pulling my gun from my coat pocket – my fingers clasping the cold handle was a real comfort to me – I opened the inner door and quietly moved into a darkened corridor at the end of which was the room where the radio was playing. The door of the room was slightly ajar and a thin yellow strip of light fell onto the dusty linoleum on the floor. As I stood and listened, I could clearly hear the voice of Jack Warner. The occupant or occupants were obviously listening to *Garrison Theatre*. At that moment I wished I were at home in front of my own hearth doing the same thing.

Stealthily I moved down the corridor towards the lighted room. On my left was the staircase leading upstairs. I heard the laughter of the radio audience supplemented by a hoarse chuckle which I deduced must belong to Bruce Horsefield. Or at least I hoped so. At this thought, my heartbeat quickened.

With gritted teeth, I swung the door open gently and surveyed the interior. It was a shabby but nonetheless cosy sitting room. Bruce Horsefield was sitting by an electric fire with his injured leg up on a stool and a glass of beer in his hand smirking away at the radio banter. So enamoured was he by the radio show that he did not at first realise another person had entered the room. Then some sixth sense made him twitch and he turned awkwardly and saw me. I held my gun clearly in view.

'Don't do anything foolish, Bruce. I want to deliver you breathing in one piece to our friends at Scotland Yard.'

Horsefield was shocked by my sudden appearance and he dropped his glass of beer, the liquid spilling on to the hearth rug. However, he soon recovered his equilibrium and shifted his wounded leg off the stool as if he intended to rise from the chair.

'Stay put,' I barked.

His eyes flamed and for a moment I thought he was going to ignore my order and that I was going to have to use my gun. My stomach juddered. I didn't want to shoot him. I didn't want to shoot any man. It's not my way.

But then strangely, he relaxed and I could almost swear that a ghost of a smile touched his lips. The odd flickering of his eyes, as though he were watching something over my shoulder, should have warned me that there was danger but it all happened so quickly that I really had no time to react.

There was a sudden violent cry worthy of a weird horror film harpy and then someone jumped on my back and clamped their scrawny arms around my neck. It did not take me long to realise that this was Mrs Horsefield – the mother.

She screamed obscenities as I swung myself round in a desperate attempt to dislodge this creature who like some fearsome piggy-backing child clung on tenaciously. Meanwhile Horsefield had risen from his chair and was advancing on me. I raised the gun.

'Stop now or I will shoot,' I cried. But as I did so, the screeching gargoyle on my back, released one of her arms and brought it down hard on my wrist. The gun spun from my grip and clattered to the floor by the hearth.

Horsefield dived for it. Within seconds the tables had turned. Now I was the one who could easily end up in the morgue.

With a grin worthy of the Cheshire cat, Horsefield rose to his feet, the gun in his hand, pointing in my direction. I could see from the cold glint in his eyes that he meant to pull the trigger. In essence, I had only seconds to live.

With a concerted effort, I swung my whole body round, heaving my shoulders upwards as far as I could push them in one enormous shrug. This violent revolution caused Mrs Horsefield to billow out, her legs swinging free. As I spun round like a whirling Dervish, her body collided heavily with her son's, knocking him to the floor. The collision caused my passenger to give a great whoop of horror. Her confusion made her release her grip and thus dislodged, she ricocheted into her son, landing on top of him.

While Bruce still held the gun, he was now flat on his back with his spindly mother spread-eagled across his frame. It was a slapstick routine worthy of Abbott and Costello. Quickly regaining my composure after my bizarre fairground ride, I stepped forward and stamped on Horsefield's wrist. He gave a yelp of pain and his fingers uncurled from around the handle of my gun.

I snatched it up and pointed it at Horsefield's head. I fired but aimed to miss. The gunshot reverberated round the room like a clap of thunder, the bullet lodging in the skirting board. My little demonstration had its desired effect. Both mother and son stopped moving and lay still, staring with apprehension at me and more particularly at the weapon I held in my hand.

'Now if either of you wish to live long enough to have another breakfast, albeit in a cell at Scotland Yard, I suggest you do exactly what I say. Understood?'

Mute nods came slowly in response.

'Right, sit together on the sofa and please, no funny business, eh? Bullets cost money, you know.'

They did as I asked like chastened children.

I knew that I would not have long to wait. I was certain that the gunshot would assure me of that.

Indeed, a couple of minutes later, I heard a frantic muffled voice calling my name and seconds later Peter burst into the room.

'Johnny,' he cried, 'are you all right. I heard a gunshot.'

'Yes, I'm fine. Just a little target practice'.

Then he saw the two characters on the sofa and grinned. 'You got him!' he cried, his face breaking into a broad grin.

'Now that you've answered my summons…' I held up the gun. 'Off you go to that phone box and call the police. 'Tell them, we've got a thief and a murderer for them.'

'You bastard,' sneered Mrs Horsefield.

I shrugged. 'Everyone's a critic.'

* * *

I got to bed very late that night, but as I lay my head on my pillow, I had a smile on my lips. Horsefield and his mother were in custody at Scotland Yard. Inspector Sullivan had organised a search of the derelict house for the morning and I had deposited the grinning Peter back at home with the Horner sisters who had been reasonably forgiving about his late arrival. A successful conclusion to my case. I hoped Father Sanderson approved.

Strangely, sleep did not come easily that night. In the darkness, my mood of gentle euphoria faded quite quickly to be replaced with an unnerving sense of disquiet. I felt as though some dark cloud was louring over me. Tired as I was, I lay awake for some time wondering why I felt so apprehensive.

TWENTY-NINE

Sheila Llewellyn played idly with her toast. She really didn't want it, but out of habit she had grilled two slices of bread and smeared them with a thin coating of margarine. Now, as she sat alone at the kitchen table, she had no desire to eat them. Her mind was far from food. She was thinking about her husband. Worrying about her husband. Well, it was part of her 'job' she supposed. When you are married to a policeman, you cannot expect to have an easy life. There were the terrible hours and the danger. The job was like a third person in the relationship. And she could read David like a barometer. He rarely discussed his work, his investigations, but she could tell by his demeanour, however much he tried to disguise it, whether things were going well or not. If the smiles were not quite as frequent and the charming worry lines on his forehead deepened, she knew David was dealing with a real stinker. When these came along, she worried all the more, as she was doing this morning.

For the last few days, David had been really low. He had hardly made any real attempt to hide it. For him that was rare, if not unique. At the thought of his tired and worried face, Sheila felt a dark cloud descend upon her. Absent-mindedly she picked up one of the slices of toast, held it for a moment and then dropped it back on the plate.

'Come on,' she said softly, chiding herself. 'This will not do.' She knew she had to be strong for the man she loved. If she showed that she was down in the dumps too, that would be an extra burden for him to carry. No, she must remain bright, cheerful and supportive whatever she was feeling inside. Surely, whatever was bringing David down would pass and he would return to his usual cheerful self. Surely?

Scooping up the pieces of toast, she dropped then into the waste bin under the sink and set about washing up. While she was drying the few items, left by herself and those much earlier by David before he had set off at dawn for the Yard, the door bell rang.

With a little puzzled frown, she dried her hands and went through to the hall to answer the door. Through the pane of frosted glass she saw the dark frame of a tall man. As she undid the latch, she wondered if it was one of David's colleagues. At this thought, a slight tremor of fear ran through her. She hoped to God that it wasn't bad news.

As soon as she opened the door she knew two things. It wasn't one of David's colleagues and she should not have opened the door.

The man who stood before her was unkempt, his shoulders hunched in a strange menacing fashion, but what was really unnerving was his rather twisted grin and the fierce malevolence in his eyes.

'Mrs Llewellyn,' he said, his voice gruff but polite.

'Yes,' she replied hesitantly.

'That's good,' he grinned, the eyes widening in pleasure and he stepped forward as if to enter the house.

Instinctively Sheila made a move to close the door on him, but she was not quick or strong enough. He forced the door back and pushed her inside.

Her instinct was to scream, but she knew that this would achieve nothing. There was no one near to come to her rescue. She did not know who this creature was or what he wanted, but she knew he was dangerous and a threat. She turned to run, but he caught her by the throat and held her.

'Please don't struggle, Mrs Llewellyn. I really don't want to hurt you. Not yet, anyway. It would be best for you and your husband if you did as I tell you.'

'My husband,' she croaked. 'What about my husband?'

'He and I have a little unfinished business to conduct.'

'What do you want with him?'

The man giggled obscenely. 'All in good time. Now if I release my grip, I want your promise not to try anything silly like trying to run away. You can't run away and if you try I shall get mad and that means I'll probably hurt you.'

The sentiments were expressed in such a matter of fact way that they filled Sheila with all-consuming dread.

'Now, are you going to be a good girl?'

'Yes,' she said.

"That's very sensible,' he grinned, releasing his grip on her throat. 'Now I've got my car outside and we're going for a little ride.'

He took her arm and pulled her towards the door. 'Now, no funny business. OK?'

She nodded, her mind whirling with desperate thoughts.

Outside, was an old Vauxhall which he'd driven up the drive right to the front door. With swift deft movements, he opened the boot. 'Step inside, my dear.'

Sheila Llewellyn looked at him with incredulity.

'Do as you're told, if you know what's good for you.' He squeezed her arm until it hurt.

Sheila was tempted to try to break free and make a bolt for it down the drive, but some instinct stopped her, told her that she wouldn't make it and then, who knows what the brute might do to her. With a sinking heart she clambered into the boot of the car.

'Lie down and curl up,' he snapped.

She did as he ordered and then darkness enveloped her as he slammed the boot lid down.

Moments later as the engine revved into life and began to judder forward, Sheila Llewellyn curled her hands into tight fists so that the nails dug into her palms and very quietly she began to cry.

* * *

'I've had word from the fire officer in charge of last night's blaze,' said Sergeant Sunderland as he wandered over to David Llewellyn's desk. His boss was staring at a pile of papers, but not really seeing them. His mind was elsewhere.

'Oh, yes,' he looked up distractedly. 'What's he got to say?'

Sunderland perched on the edge of the desk. 'Apparently they did find a body in the shell of the house this morning. Or to be more precise the remains of a body. It's too far gone to be any use to us. Apparently they can't even tell if it's a man or a woman.'

'Great.'

'Just some bones and ash.'

'So we don't know if it's Sexton or not,'

'Well, it was his house.'

Llewellyn shook his head. 'That proves nothing. There's something fishy about this affair. Look at the facts. Sexton visits Northcote on a regular basis in the loony bin on the premise of writing a book about criminal madness or some such. Suddenly Northcote escapes – very easily it seems – and disappears. And strangely Sexton seems unable to explain Northcote's behaviour or to help us in anyway. In fact, his lack of assistance was in essence a hindrance.'

'Then the murders begin,' added Sunderland.

'Yes... in the same manner as before. And then we find Sexton's cigarette case at the scene of the most recent atrocity. You know what I wonder, Sunderland, don't you?'

Sunderland threw his boss a quizzical look. 'Not sure.'

'I wonder if these two were in cahoots. I mean it's a fairly unhealthy pursuit to keep visiting a cannibal murderer, isn't it? Perhaps Sexton developed a curiosity about the killings… about the ritual of eating flesh. Maybe he wanted to try them out for himself.'

Sunderland grimaced. 'It's enough to turn your stomach.'

'Your stomach, yes, 'cause you're a straight forward pie and chips man, but to some twisted minds like Northcote … and maybe Sexton… it's lovely grub.'

Sunderland grimaced again. 'You're putting me right off my lunch.'

Llewellyn afforded himself a little smile at his sergeant's discomfort. 'Well, whether they were working together or not, we are still no nearer catching either of them. And, I hate to admit this, but I've no idea what we're going to do next. We seem to be up that creek without a bleedin' paddle.'

With this dark admission, both men fell silent. At length, Sunderland roused himself. 'Shall I make us both a cuppa?'

'Why not?' sighed Llewellyn. 'It might help invigorate the brain cells.'

Sunderland had only just left the office when the telephone rang. David casually lifted the receiver, 'Llewellyn,' he said.

There was a pause before the caller spoke. 'Good morning, Inspector. This is Dr Ralph Northcote.'

David's body stiffened and a little electric charge seem to run up his backbone. He sat bolt upright in his chair, gripping the phone hard enough to snap the receiver in two.

'Oh, yes…' he found himself saying, his words escaping somewhat muffled from a dry mouth.

'Oh, I assure you I am Ralph Northcote. This is not a hoax call. Surely you remember my voice… from before.'

David thought he did. 'What can I do for you?' he said as casually as he could.

Northcote chuckled. 'It's more a case of what I can do for

you. You see I have your wife… but I really don't want your wife, I want you.'

'Sheila…' stuttered Llewellyn, fear and apprehension fogging his brain.

'Yes, little Sheila. Blonde-haired Sheila. I have her.'

David shook his head in disbelief. Was this maniac telling the truth or was it some cruel, wild bluff?

'I called on her this morning and persuaded her to come away with me. She was not too keen at first, but you know I have my little ways of persuasion.'

'Bastard.'

'Of course. That goes without saying.'

'If you have hurt her…'

'Oh, please, don't trot out the impotent threats. If I have hurt her… there is nothing you can do about it, Inspector. However, I have not hurt her. Really, I have no interest in hurting her, although I am sure her flesh is quite tasty…'

David's stomach lurched and he wanted to bellow a stream of obscenities down the phone at his tormentor, but his wiser nature told him that not only would it not help the situation but it might make it worse.

'What do you want?'

'I want you. I want to do a swap. You for your wife.'

'Very well.'

'I thought you would agree. But you must obey my instructions to the letter or I will slit dear Sheila's throat and prepare myself a very tasty snack. Is that understood?'

For a brief moment, David wondered if this were really happening. Was it just a bad dream? A cruel nightmare from which he would wake any second. But as he stared unseeingly at the black telephone he knew in his heart that it was real. Very real.

'What do you want me to do?'

'You tell no one – no one about this call. Your colleagues

must not know. You are in this on your own. Is that clear?

'Yes.'

'At six o'clock this evening, you will be on the corner of Horseferry Road and Millbank by the Lambeth Bridge down by the river. There is a telephone box there. I will ring you and give you further instructions. I cannot emphasise enough that no one must know of this arrangement and you must come alone. Failure to comply with these instructions and… well, it's goodbye Sheila. Is that understood?'

'Yes.'

'Do as you are told and your wife lives. Act foolishly and… well you know the consequences.'

The line went dead.

For some moments David Llewellyn sat like a frozen statue, his hand still gripping the telephone receiver in his hand, his heart thumping in his chest. Suddenly he became conscious of a trickle of sweat travelling down his cheek from his temple. He slammed the receiver down savagely and grabbed a handkerchief from his trouser pocket and mopped his face.

'Tea up,' cried Sergeant Sunderland, breezing into the room carrying two mugs and plonking one down on David's desk.

Automatically, he picked up the mug and took a sip of the hot tea.

'So, what do we do next, sir?' said Sunderland, returning to his usual perch on the end of the desk.

David desperately tried to force his scrambled brain into functioning normally. When he eventually spoke, he found that his voice emerged in a strange mechanical fashion reminiscent of a speak your weight machine.

'I'm… I'm not sure. Things… are a bit … desperate. Look, Sunderland, why don't you take a trip to Sexton's surgery and… have a snoop round his office… his files. See if you can come up with something.'

Sunderland looked his boss with some concern. He seemed odd somehow. His face was white and damp with sweat and he was talking in an weird way.

'Are you all right, sir?'

'I feel a bit queasy. Probably a dodgy sausage I had for... breakfast. Anyway, you get off and see what you can sniff out at Sexton's surgery, eh?'

'I can finish my tea first, can't I?'

Llewellyn forced a smile. It almost hurt him. 'Of course. As for me, I've got a little lead I'd like to follow up.' Without a further word, he snatched his hat and coat from the rack and left the room.

Sunderland gazed at the full mug of tea, untouched, on his boss's desk and raised his brow in surprise.

'Now what's got into him?'

* * *

Twenty minutes later, David Llewellyn was in the bathroom at home, his head over the toilet bowl. He had just relieved himself of his breakfast, including the supposedly dodgy sausage. His stomach was now empty, but he was still retching, his ashen face bathed in sweat.

On leaving the Yard, he had telephoned home, hoping against hope that Sheila would pick up the receiver at the other end. But it just rang and rang. And rang. He had then driven like the devil back to his house trying but failing to block out all the dark and despondent thoughts which were desperate to crowd in and taunt him.

On arriving home and finding the door ajar, his worst nightmare was confirmed. He carried out a cursory search of the house but knew he would find nothing. Northcote had been telling the truth. He had Sheila in his bloody clutches. It was then that the overpowering sense of nausea overcame him and he rushed to the lavatory to be sick.

After a while, he rose from his crouching posture and washed his face and swilled his mouth out with cold water. As he gazed at his haunted face in the bathroom mirror, one question above all pounded in his mind, thundered repeatedly in his brain like the stroke of a blacksmith's hammer. What was he going to do? What was he going to do?

THIRTY

I was in business again! The following morning after my adventures with the Horsefield family, I was visited by a new client. Time was when such a small, rather sordid case of suspected adultery would have seemed small beer and depressed me, but after the several empty 'feeling sorry for myself' months, to get a regular client seemed wonderful. Normality seemed to be rearing its head again. It was a remarkable feeling and I am sure Max would have been pleased for me. I blew a kiss to her picture on my desk.

I was just lighting a celebratory cigarette when the telephone rang. Wow, I thought, not another client? I was wrong.

It was David Llewellyn.

* * *

I met him in The Guardsman at noon and we secured one of the little private booths at the rear of the saloon bar. Here, away from the noise and the smoke we were afforded a little privacy. My friend looked terrible. His face was grey as though all the blood had been drained from it and his skin had a damp sheen to it. His eyes blinked nervously as he raised his pint glass to his lips.

I knew something was wrong – very wrong. I had deduced that from the tone of his voice and his strange manner during the telephone call. He had told me nothing, only that he needed to see me urgently. David never asked to see me urgently.

'What's this all about?' I asked casually, eager to get the ball rolling.

David ran his hand over his face. 'It's this Northcote case.'

'Northcote. Mr Cannibal?'

David nodded. 'He's got Sheila.'

'What do you…?'

'What the hell do you think I mean? He's got Sheila. He's abducted her.'

'My God!' I said, my mind filling up with questions, only to ask the one that I shouldn't.

'Are you sure?'

'Of course I'm bloody sure!' His eyes widened in anger and his hand shook so much, the beer slopped over the side of the glass.

I touched the sleeve of his coat with what I hoped was a reassuring gesture. 'Tell me about it.'

David took a large gulp of beer before responding. 'He came to the house this morning after I'd gone to work and… took her. Then he rang me at the Yard. He said he'll let her go in exchange for me.'

'Exchange. A kind of swap?'

'He wants revenge. I was the copper who nabbed him in the first place. I'm the one responsible for getting him locked away for life. Now he intends to get his own back. I'm supposed to be in a phone box down by Lambeth Bridge on the Millbank side at six this evening and he'll give me more instructions. Where to go. Where to meet him. Once he's got me, he'll let Sheila go.'

Like hell he will, I thought but knew now was not the time to air such an opinion. Instead, I said nothing.

'The problem is,' he continued after another gulp of beer, 'there has to be no police involvement. I've got to do this on my own or else… or else he'll slit Sheila's throat.'

'But you can't do this without a surveillance team to help.'

'I can't risk it, Johnny. If he gets a whiff of a police presence… I just can't risk it. I've got to do it on his terms… for Sheila's sake'. There was a catch in his voice and he turned his head away momentarily while he brought his emotions in check.

I wanted to say all kinds of sympathetic, reassuring and encouraging words but I was well aware this is not what David wanted to hear just now. Besides, I knew I would struggle to make them sound convincing. In truth, my old friend was in a no-win situation. How can you take the word of a mad killer as gospel? This Northcote creature may well have killed Sheila already; if not, he wasn't going to release her when he'd got his hands on David. What fun he could have torturing Sheila while David was forced to watch. Or vice versa. My heart sank at the thought of this impossible situation. I knew that David was an experienced and intelligent enough policeman to be fully aware, as I was, of the drastic implications of this terrible scenario. His face clearly indicated that this knowledge was tearing him apart. And there was nothing I could say that would alter the situation.

'I need your help', he said quietly but forcefully.

I did not have to think about a reply.

'Of course. Whatever I can do.'

'I need you as my shadow tonight. Even if the bastard gets me, perhaps you'll be able to get him.'

* * *

Later that afternoon, I sat hunched over my desk, staring into space, both hands grasping a mug of coffee. I was miserable and I could not believe it. I had started the day with a brightening of the spirit. After the dark months after Max's death, I felt I was reaching for the light again – normality at least. I had completed the case for Father Sanderson and I'd got myself back on the detective treadmill. Things were looking up. And then came the hammer blow. I had just lost the love of my life and now one of my friends, a man who has been so good to me, was in great danger of losing his.

Whoever was in charge of our Fate up there needed a good kick in the crotch.

I broke my reverie to glance at my watch. It was only three thirty. Time goes so slowly when you are waiting. I had great forebodings about that evening's venture. I did not know how it could end happily. I chided myself for being so negative but the feeling of dark apprehension would not go away.

On leaving David at lunchtime, I had gone along to Barry Forshaw's garage to hire a motor for the evening. If I was going to follow David, I needed my own set of wheels. Certainly shank's pony would not do and equally the situation was far too dangerous and uncertain for me to rely on the services of a taxi driver. Barry was an old client of mine. I had extricated him from a forged number plate business when he'd gone in too far. With my help, we exposed the gang and I managed to get Barry a reduced sentence for helping with the arrests and turning King's evidence. He's been grateful ever since.

'I have a nice little roadster, you can have,' he said, leading me into the compound at the back of the garage. The motor certainly looked smart and nippy, but just a little too individual and therefore too noticeable. I needed something that would blend in with the stream of traffic and not catch anyone's eye. An ordinary motor.

'What about the Wolseley?' I asked, moving over to a shabby-looking vehicle.

'That old thing. It's been around the block a few times, I can tell you.'

'Just the kind of crock I'm after. It is roadworthy, I suppose.'

Barry grinned at my impertinence. 'Certainly,' he said, with feigned irritation. 'I don't deal in any other kind of motor car.'

'Good. Then I'll take it. How much?'

'Bring it back in the morning without a scratch on it and a full tank of petrol. How about that?'

'You got a deal.' We shook hands.

The car was a bit clunky, but so am I as a driver. I'm in control of a car so infrequently that I remain as rusty at the steering wheel as the mudguards on this old jalopy. I hoped that I was up to my duties for this evening. I drove around for about an hour getting used to the controls and feel of the vehicle before heading home. It certainly was a sturdy drive. Driving this for a month would certainly develop one's arm muscles.

I drained my coffee mug, lit a cigarette, and glanced at my watch again. The hands had hardly moved.

Would this evening ever come?

Suddenly the rumbling of my tummy alerted me to the fact that I hadn't eaten anything since breakfast and that consisted of a cup of tea, a scrappy piece of toast and a fag. I needed some grub to help sustain me through the ordeal tonight. I decided to pop down to Benny's and treat myself to one of his specials. I smiled at the thought. Knowing Benny's cooking it would hardly be a treat and it certainly wouldn't be special, but at least it would be warm and I'd have a chance to see the old boy. I felt sure that his banter would help lighten my mood temporarily before setting out off on my evening adventure.

As I pulled up in the Wolseley outside Benny's café, I saw him peering through the window and he caught sight of me as I got out of the car.

'Up the world we've come, Mr Rolls Royce!' was his greeting as I entered.

'It's an old Wolseley and it's on loan for the night. It goes back in the morning.'

'A Cinderella motorist, eh? You got a special date with that lovely Russian girl.'

I grinned. I knew Benny would cheer me up.

'You could say that,' I lied. I certainly didn't want to tell Benny the real reason for hiring the motor.

I ordered the special of the day and a pot of tea and took a seat by the window. Five minutes later Benny delivered the goods – a plate of liver and onions accompanied by a greyish splodge of mashed potato.

'I must say that you are looking a little more like your old self, Johnny. But you still need feeding up.'

'You said I needed feeding up when you first met me five years ago.'

Benny chuckled. 'Yes I did.'

'I'm fine, Benny. I'm back in the saddle and I've almost stopped feeling sorry for myself. When you get a blow like I did – losing Max so suddenly in such a terrible way – you think you're the only one going through hell. It numbs you to other's pain. So many people are suffering in this bloody war...' I paused, my knife and fork motionless over the food, the image of David Llewellyn's drained and tortured face shimmered before me. Suddenly I didn't feel hungry any more.

'Loss is always with you, Johnny. A day doesn't go by when I don't think about my Daisy, but you learn, you learn to cope with it. And you get on with your life. It's what they would have wanted.'

I prayed that this wasn't a lesson that David would have to learn.

THIRTY-ONE

In her dark tomb, Sheila Llewellyn had lost track of time. She had no idea how long she had been incarcerated in the boot of this maniac's vehicle. Initially, she had curled up foetal-like – like a frightened child, but gradually her fear had subsided and a kind of numbness of mind came to her, almost an anaesthetic, removing the pain of reality. At one point, when the vehicle had parked, she had actually fallen asleep.

The car was on the move once more, and it swayed and shook violently as though it was being driven at great speed. And recklessly. Suddenly a thought struck Sheila, Perhaps he never intended to let her out ever again. She was meant to die here, to lose consciousness through lack of food and water and then rot. She would be found months later – a rotting corpse. She shuddered at the thought but somehow she was glad to have considered such an outcome. Facing the worst in some strange way gave her courage and hope.

The vehicle slowed and ground to a halt. After a moment, she heard the driver's door slam and then the key in the lock of the boot. Seconds later, the boot lid was raised slowly. Sheila screwed up her eyes as the blinding daylight flooded in.

And then a shadow fell over her.

'The circular tour is over,' her captor observed. 'Time to leave'. He reached into the boot and grabbed Sheila's arm. 'Come on,' he said gruffly.

Her body was stiff and awkward and her limbs failed to obey her. He dragged her over the edge of the boot and she fell forward, her hands hitting the harsh gravel. With some effort, she pulled herself forward until her legs flopped to the ground also. She lay there like a landed fish on a riverbank.

'Welcome home,' sneered Northcote, once more clamping his hand around Sheila's right arm and hauling her to her feet. Her vision blurred, she felt nauseous for some moments and then gradually her surroundings came into focus. Her mouth opened in shock. Sheila couldn't believe it. She was back home. She was in her own drive. The car was almost in the same position it had been when she had been bundled into it those long hours ago. Was this some kind of cruel hoax?

Her eyes and expression must have clearly mirrored her thoughts and Northcote laughed at her confusion.

'I've brought you back home, to wait for hubby to return. We're going to have a cosy evening together.'

'What the hell are you talking about?' Sheila was surprised at the ferocity and the volume of her retort. Frustration, confusion and desperation had commingled to make her very angry. So angry in fact that she lashed out with her foot, kicking Northcote in the leg.

He gave a cry of surprise and staggered back. Sheila was tempted to kick him again and this time aim at somewhere more vulnerable, but instead she turned and ran. Passing down the edge of the car, she headed down the drive for the gate.

She hadn't been prepared for the awkwardness of her body. Cooped up in virtually one position for many hours, it was learning to function again. Her limbs were stiff and did not automatically obey her. She ran like someone who has severe arthritis travelling over a bed of hot coals.

Within seconds, Northcote was upon her and brought her to the ground. She crashed onto the hard gravel.

'Naughty, naughty,' he gasped. 'I see that I shall have to

watch you. Now get up.'

Reluctantly she did so.

'That's a good girl,' he said, and marched her back down the drive. After retrieving a small case from the back seat of the car and then he dragged Sheila into the house.

'Can I have a drink of water, please?' she asked.

'Another trick?'

'No, no. I am very thirsty.'

Northcote pulled a knife from his pocket. He held the shiny bright blade in front of Sheila's face. 'I don't want to cut you just yet, Mrs Llewellyn, but if I have any more trouble from you, I'm afraid I will have to slit your throat. Is that understood?'

Sheila shivered with fear and nodded vigorously, words failing her at this moment.

Northcote took her into the kitchen where she filled a glass of water from the tap and gulped it down eagerly.

'Now it's time to secure you for the evening. We must have you ready and nicely trussed for when hubby comes home?'

'What... what are you going to do?'

'Oh, that's a surprise. You like surprises, don't you?'

At knife point, he took her upstairs. When he led her into the bedroom, she feared the worst. She determined that if he was going to try and sexually molest her she would kick, scream and bite like a demon. She would rather be knifed to death than succumb to his advances. He would not violate her without a damn struggle.

But it seemed that Northcote had other ideas.

Opening his case, he took out several lengths of rope and a reel of strong tape.

'Time to truss up the turkey,' he observed with a grin.

Sheila actually felt a sense of relief when she realised that this maniac only intended to tie her up rather than rape her.

She offered no resistance as he bound her feet and tied her hands behind her back. Then he rolled off a strip of tape, cut it with his knife and placed it across her mouth. As he did this she tried to scream but the tape prevented the sound escaping.

'You'll have to breathe through your nose for a while, my dear.' Northcote chuckled to himself. He was really enjoying this grotesque charade. 'And now a final touch,' he added as he thrust her onto the bed. Snatching up a pillowcase, he detached the pillow and slipped the empty case over Sheila's head.

'That should keep you nice and quiet until your hubby arrives,' he said, standing back and admiring his handiwork.

Sheila lay on the bed, engulfed in darkness and began to sob softly.

Northcote left her to her misery. Locking the bedroom door he went down stairs and checked his watch. It was almost time to set off. His features broke into a broad smile. He was going to enjoy this evening. Who was it who said revenge was a dish best served cold?

THIRTY-TWO

David Llewellyn arrived at Lambeth Bridge early. He was terrified that if he did not obey Northcote's instructions to the letter, he would be placing Sheila's life in jeopardy. Or, as he grimly reconsidered, more jeopardy than it already was – if that were possible. His mind was all over the place and his stomach was spinning like a top. He was sure that he was going to be sick at any moment.

The day was on the brink of evening and a stiff breeze blew off the river. Instinctively, he pulled his overcoat around him, although he was fully aware that it wasn't the cool air that was making him shiver. It was fear. Fear that whatever he did this evening, the outcome would be tragic.

At quarter past six, he approached the telephone box, which was on the opposite side of the road to the bridge. As he did so, he gazed around him as casually as he was able in order to see if he could spot Johnny anywhere.

He couldn't.

This did not dismay him too much. He that knew Johnny wouldn't let him down. Would he? No, of course not. He prayed that he wouldn't anyway.

The phone box was occupied. A large woman with a shopping bag was in full flow. David checked his watch. Still ten minutes to go. That was all right. As long as this woman finished soon.

For a moment, he had a vision of him swinging open the door of the box and hauling her out mid-sentence, so that he could receive his call on time.

Crazy thought. He mopped his brow. He hoped it was a crazy thought. God, he could do with a drink, but that was the last thing on earth he should have now. He knew that he needed a clear head to deal with the unknown events ahead of him; at least as clear as he could make it. Alcohol would only slow his reactions, muffle his thinking and take the edge off his reactions.

He mopped his brow again and stared into the box as the woman oblivious of his presence rattled on. Once again he gazed around him as casually and as nonchalantly as he could, hoping to catch a glimpse of Johnny. He still couldn't. In his fraught state he didn't know whether this was a good thing or bad. If Johnny was performing a brilliant chameleon trick, that was fine. He just hoped that he was actually out there watching, for without his aid, he was a goner and indeed so was Sheila. At the thought of his wife, David's stomach lurched once more.

He was just about to reach inside his jacket for a cigarette, when the large lady emerged from the phone box. She passed him without a glance and crossed the road and headed for the bridge.

David hauled open the door and squeezed himself inside. It was like being in an acrid smelling womb... or coffin. Now he just had to wait. Just had to wait for the next move in this deadly game. He stared at the black bakelite telephone crouching there like a wary spider. How long would it be before it rang?

God, a thought struck him. What if it didn't ring? What if this were some cruel hoax? What if Northcote had set this up, just to buy himself some time? What if he'd already murdered Sheila and was now miles away from London?

What a fool he'd been.

He felt faint and began to sweat profusely. The walls of the telephone box seemed to press in on him and felt claustrophobic.

'Ring,' he croaked addressing the telephone. 'For God's sake ring.'

But the phone remained silent.

The minutes ticked by and David's anxiety grew. At one point he lifted the receiver to see if it was actually working. The reverberating burr that emerged from the earpiece told him that it was.

He dropped the receiver back in the cradle as though it had caught fire. He didn't want the telephone to register an engaged tone and miss the call.

But the call did not come.

He checked his watch. The minute hand was crawling up towards twenty to seven.

'Oh, my god, it is a trick' he cried softly. 'A bloody cruel joke.'

And then suddenly the door of the telephone box swung open and someone forced their way inside.

'Good evening, Inspector,' said Ralph Northcote, a nasty grin plastered on his face. He held up a knife so that David could see it. 'One silly move and you get this right between the ribs. Is that understood?'

'Where's Sheila?'

'Oh, she's quite safe for the moment. And will remain so, as long as you do exactly what I tell you to do. Is that understood?'

David nodded, the sweat now running profusely down his face and he felt faint. What, he wondered, had this mad man got in mind – what nasty plan had he got up his sleeve?

'I trust that you have brought no weapon with you. Nothing concealed somewhere?'

'No.'

Northcote patted his jacket, coat pockets and felt down the legs of his trousers. 'Mmm,' he said, 'you seem to be telling the truth.'

'I am, I swear.'

'Good man. Now when we step out of this box, we shall turn right and round into Thorne Street. You'll see a Vauxhall car there. We shall stand behind it and I will open the boot and we'll look inside as though inspecting something in there. When the coast is clear, you'll climb inside.

'But...'

Northcote pressed the knife against David's ribs. 'No questions, Mr Policeman. Do as I say or else...'

Northcote pushed his weight against the door of the telephone box and with an eerie creak it swung open. 'You walk before me and, please, don't try anything heroic. Remember, I have the knife and I know where your wife is.'

David stepped ahead of Northcote onto the pavement and walked slowly in the direction that he had been instructed to take. As he did so, he gazed around him as inconspicuously as he could in the desperate hope of seeing Johnny. There was no sign of him whatsoever,

They turned into Thorne Street and he saw Northcote's car.

Northcote moved bedside him and opened the boot.

'Lean forward and inspect the interior,' he said.

David did as he was told.

Northcote gazed around the quiet street. Dusk was falling and there were no pedestrians or traffic. The time was ripe.

'Right, get into the boot,' he snapped

David climbed over the edge of the boot and hunched his body in order to fit in the confined space.

Suddenly darkness fell as the boot lid came down. He was trapped in an airless dark bubble. And he was helpless.

Outside, he could hear the dark satanic laughter of his captor.

THIRTY-THREE

I left Benny's café just as he was about to shut up shop for the day. He came on to the pavement with me to inspect the motor car. He pulled a face on seeing the vehicle close up.

'Beggars can't be choosers, I suppose,' he said. 'But this old crock is like me: it's seen better days.'

'It gets me from A to B,' I said with a smile.

'But what if you want to go further?'

It was a good question. One that I could not answer.

I clambered into the cab, wound down the window, gave a quick wave and turned the ignition to start up the engine. It resisted my first attempt and indeed my second, but with further coaxing and a little extra choke, it spluttered into life on the third go.

'I think it's time you gave it back to the circus,' said Benny, as I pulled away in a manner far more stately than I had hoped.

I glanced at my watch. It was ten to six. I reckoned it would take me about twenty minutes to get to Lambeth Bridge. I would be in plenty of time to witness David's telephone call.

Or so I thought.

It soon became obvious that the car thought otherwise. I was just passing down Redcliffe Gardens on my way to the Embankment when a strange gurgling and hissing noise emanated from the bonnet. This was quickly followed by a violent jerking motion before the car juddered to a silent halt. I turned the ignition desperately, but the engine did not respond. 'What the hell!' I thought, as I jumped out onto the pavement and gazed impotently at the dead animal. What on earth was I going to do? My knowledge of the internal combustion engine was less than nil. I didn't even know how to raise the damned bonnet. Out of frustration, I kicked the front wheel. This action was not only of no practical use but it didn't make me feel any better either.

'A spot of bother?'

I turned to face the owner of the voice who stood a few feet behind me. He was a tall, distinguished looking gentleman in a smart dark overcoat and a bowler hat. He had well chiselled aristocratic features, bright blue eyes and a well trimmed jaunty moustache which was now white with age.

'The thing has died on me.'

'Did it splutter, steam and then shudder to a stop?'

I raised my eyebrows in surprise. 'That's about the size of it.'

His pale face split into a smile.

'The old ones often do. These Wolseleys are nice little runners in their youth, but I'm afraid time does wither them and spoil their infinite reliability. But fear not. It will be dirt in the carburettor. It always is. As they get older and worn, these motors let in all sorts of alien smut. I should know; I had one of these for nearly eight years. I was sorry to see it go. Open her up. We'll soon sort the old girl out'.

I shook my head. 'I'm sorry, I've no idea how to do that. Open up the bonnet, I mean.'

'My, you are a novice. Are you sure you're fit to drive this beauty.'

On the evidence so far, I didn't think I was. But then again, she was hardly a beauty either.

The old gentleman led me round to the driver's side, opened the door and reached inside. 'See, here, there's a lever,' he said in the manner of a friendly school teacher. 'This releases the catch on the bonnet.' He gave the lever a sharp tug and the bonnet responded with gentle snap.

My mentor lifted up the bonnet and leaned over, peering beneath the canopy. He hummed a little as he inspected the interior and then dipped his hands inside. Heaven knows what he was doing, but he seemed to be doing it with supreme confidence.

'Just as I thought,' he said at last. 'Dirty carburettor. Well, dirty and decrepit, if the truth be known. It really needs renewing. It's on its last legs. Have you an old rag?'

'I'm not sure,' I mumbled and inspected the inside of the car for such an item without success. I dug into my pocket and pulled out my handkerchief. 'Will this do?'

The old gentleman gave a sad shake of the head. It was clear that he thought I wasn't fit to be in charge of this motor car – a man who has no idea how to open the bonnet and does not even possess an old piece of rag to wipe up spills and smears.

'You'll not be able to use this handkerchief again,' he said, returning to the task of doing something under the bonnet.

As he did so, I gazed at my watch. It was six fifteen. Time was running out, but I could hardly tell the old fellow to hurry up. He was doing me a great favour after all. A favour to an incompetent ignoramus of a motorist.

After a few moments, he stood clear of the car. 'That should do it', he said, handing me my handkerchief back. It was now thick with soot and grease. I threw it on the floor of the car.

'Give the engine a try,' he said cheerily. For a moment I thought he was about to add, 'You do know how to do that, don't you?' and although I suspect he was tempted, he restrained himself. I sat in the driver's seat and turned the ignition. The car whirred and whined for a moment and then remarkably coughed its way into life.

The old gentleman beamed and he slapped down the bonnet. 'There you are,' he said. 'They only need a little care and attention and they'll serve you well. I recommend that you have her serviced pronto and get the garage to replace the carburettor. That done, it'll keep going for a few years yet.'

'I don't know how to thank you,' I said, reaching for my wallet.

Spotting this gesture, he held up his hand. 'No, no. I don't need thanks. It was a pleasure for me to get my hands on one of these old machines again. I don't get a chance these days. It's shank's pony for me now. It was my pleasure.' He patted the bonnet affectionately. 'Goodbye, sir, and happy motoring.'

Without another word he walked off stiffly down the street with a jaunty gait.

I did not wait until my mechanical good Samaritan had disappeared into the throng of pedestrians, before revving up my old jalopy and driving off at speed. My watch informed me that I had less than ten minutes to reach Lambeth Bridge.

I could hear the sonorous tones of Big Ben striking the half hour as I raced down Horseferry Road, my heart beating like a rumba band and a fine sheen of sweat on my brow. At the junction with Millbank, I pulled in at the kerb and jumped out. I soon clocked the telephone box across the road and there was someone inside. From where I was standing I could not make out whether it was David or not. With as much nonchalance as I could muster, I crossed the road and made my way towards the box. As I sauntered past, I saw, to my relief, that the occupant was indeed David. I hadn't missed him. I sent up another prayer of thanks to my mechanical good Samaritan.

I returned to my car and sat inside watching the box.

Time moved on, but David remained where he was. Was it a very long call or no call at all? Was the whole thing a trick? Only time would bring the answers; all I could do was sit and wait.

And then at about twenty to seven, a heavily built man approached the telephone box and entered. His actions were so deliberate and calculated, that it was clear to me that he knew that David was in there. My God, I thought, it's Northcote. He's come in person for David. There was to be no phone call. My mind was a whirl. What was I to do? Attempting to rescue David from this situation would bring its own problems. Northcote still had Sheila somewhere and we had to find out where.

After a while the door of the telephone box opened and David and Northcote emerged. They walked slowly across the road towards the bridge and then stopped at the rear of a car. Northcote opened the boot, said something to David who then appeared to be inspecting inside it. He leaned forward so that half his body disappeared from view. Then to my horror, I saw that he clambered inside the boot and Northcote with a triumphant gesture slammed the lid down imprisoning my friend.

Gazing around him briefly to see if he had been observed, he got in the car. Immediately, I switched on my engine and revved up. I must not lose this monster: two people's lives depended on me.

As Northcote pulled away from the curb into the thin stream of traffic, I shot forward at some speed so that by the time we were across the bridge I was only one car away from him.

Luckily for me, Northcote did not seem to be in a hurry and he drove at a moderate speed. This was reassuring for it meant that he had no idea that he was being followed.

We passed the Oval cricket ground and headed in the direction of Kennington and the maze of domestic avenues in this area. Northcote had just turned down one of these streets when it happened. Or to be more precise: it happened again. The strange gurgling and hissing sound under the bonnet returned with even greater ferocity than before. This then was followed by the strange juddering motion of the whole vehicle. Suddenly, I was driving a bucking bronco. These gyrations were a brief precursor to the whole machine gasping to a full stop. Obviously, my mechanical good Samaritan had only managed a temporary repair.

I pulled the little lever to release the bonnet and peered inside. There was no way I was going to be able to repair the fault this time. I could not even identify the carburettor.

I swore. Northcote's car had disappeared from sight. I had lost him. And I had lost any chance of saving David and his wife from fates that were unimaginable.

THIRTY-FOUR

David lay in the back of the swaying vehicle in a cramped foetal position. He had never felt as helpless in his life. He had no idea where he was being taken or what fate was in store for him. He was fairly sure that Johnny was not on his tail. There had been no sign of him when he and Northcote had left the phone box. Only a bloody miracle could save him and Sheila now and as he wasn't the least bit religious, he didn't believe in miracles.

After about fifteen minutes, Northcote's car came to a stop. David could hear the scrunch of tyres on gravel as it did so. He waited in tense anticipation for the boot lid to rise, for the evening light to flood in and for Northcote to release him from his cramped prison. But nothing happened.

He banged on the boot lid but there was no response.

There was no response, because Northcote had gone into the house. He wanted to check on his prisoner inside first, to be certain that everything was as he had left it. He opened the bedroom door and saw that Sheila was lying on the floor. She obviously had made some desperate attempt to free herself of her bonds and in doing so had toppled off the bed. He found this amusing and chuckled in response.

Sheila, still hooded with the pillow case aware of a presence in the room wriggled and made a gagging sound but because of the tape across her mouth the words were indistinguishable.

Northcote pulled the pillow away from her head and lifted Sheila back onto the bed. Her eyes were wide with fear and wet from crying. This also pleased Northcote. Inducing fear was always a delight to him. He smiled as he ran the back of his hand down her cheek.

'Not long now,' he said softly.

Sheila gave a croak of fear.

'Now you stay there like a good girl and then I'll give you a big surprise. One I'm sure you'll like.'

His smile broadened as he left the room. He was pleased with himself. This was all going rather well, he thought. He couldn't remember when he had felt so happy, so fulfilled. And soon, he was sure, he would feel even happier when he was cutting up the flesh of Mr and Mrs Llewellyn.

* * *

In the sitting room, he poured himself a drink and lit a cigarette. With a sigh of pleasure, he slumped in an armchair. A moment's relaxation, contemplation before the fun of the evening. But he was too excited to relax fully. He stubbed the cigarette out before it was half-smoked and he abandoned the drink after only a few sips. He really wanted to get on with the show.

It was quite dark out now. The moon was hidden by clouds and there were few stars visible; it was only the lights from the house that dimly illuminated the drive way and the car. Knife in hand, Northcote raised the lid of the boot. The sight that met his eyes made him gasp and almost drop his weapon.

The boot was empty.

* * *

After the car had been standing silent for some minutes, David called out. At the top of his voice, he bellowed out the word, 'Help!' several times. The word reverberated dully in the airless confined space. There was no response. No rescue. But then again there was no attempt to silence him. Northcote must have left him for some reason – abandoned him.

That was good news.

Somehow David knew he had to take advantage of this hiatus. He reckoned that Northcote would not leave him there for long and so he had to do something quickly. David swivelled his body round in the cramped space so that he had his back against the inside of the boot lid and his feet were pressing on the partition between the boot and the rear seats. With as much force and as much leverage as he could muster he began kicking this partition with both feet. Surely, he thought, it cannot be that secure. At first his blows met with strong resistance, but he persisted, aiming at different portions of the partition to gauge which was likely to be the weakest. Then at last he heard a slick crack, a kind of tearing sound.

Bingo!

In the darkness, he grinned and renewed his efforts.

Slowly but with a pleasing surety, the partition began to give way.

The more he was able to drive it forward, the greater the force he was able to use to break down this barrier. Finally, with a satisfying crack, David's particular wall of Jericho came tumbling down. The seat fell forward providing a jagged aperture through to the rear of the car.

He swivelled his body round, and like a burrowing mole, pushed his way through. Within seconds he had clambered over into the front seat and was out of the car.

He stood briefly to catch his breath and fill his lungs with the cool evening air. And then, as he gazed around, he was amazed to find himself in his own driveway. He was back home. What the hell? For a moment, he thought he was having an hallucination, but a movement inside the house brought him rapidly to his senses. It was probably Northcote coming for him. He dodged to the side of the door of the house out of sight and waited.

* * *

The boot was empty. Northcote leaned forward and saw the gaping, damaged partition – his prisoner's escape route.

'You won't find me in there,' said a voice behind him.

THIRTY-FIVE

I swore again and to ease my frustration further I kicked the bumper of the accursed car. Both actions did not really help my sense of despair – and I hurt my foot in the process. Foolishly, in desperation, I looked under the bonnet once more. It was pointless. I certainly couldn't work the conjuring trick that the bowler-hatted gentleman had performed so niftily and effectively. Clean the carburettor or whatever he'd done. Perhaps I should have watched him carefully and then I could try to mimic his actions. I should have taken Barry Forshaw's advice and taken the little sporty number. I bet that little thing wouldn't have let me down, like this old crate. For a few seconds my mind whirled around such stupid thoughts while my heart thumped desperately within my breast. A little confused, I may have been, but I was fully aware how desperate and apparently hopeless my situation was. What on earth was I going to do?

The road was quiet. There was no traffic. No motorist chugging by whom I could flag down and persuade to give me a lift. Give me a lift? Where on earth to?

I had no idea.

Then my eyes fell upon the road name plate on the wall opposite. Sycamore Rise.

They lingered on it for a while and then a certain dim recognition came to me. Sycamore Rise.

Sycamore Rise!

The name reverberated in the cobwebbed passages of my memory. I knew that name. Somehow. I had heard it before. Where? How?

I was aware of the phrase 'to cudgel your brains' before

but I'd never really known what it meant – or the real effect of it until that moment. Here I was on a dark spring evening staring at a road sign, repeating it over and over again, cudgelling my tired brains in an attempt to remember…

Sycamore Rise.

It was a misnomer as the road did not 'rise' perceptively and certainly from where I was standing there were no sycamores in view. This was an observation that I'd had before. Sycamore Rise – silly name, I'd thought.

Of course!

The cudgelling had worked. It came back to me. I had been down this road before. And, yes, suddenly I knew that it led into Chestnut Avenue from which one could reach Oak Road and from thence one could turn down Larch Close.

And Larch Close was where Detective Inspector David Llewellyn lived! I could see it now in my mind's eye: a very smart modern villa situated down a long tree-lined drive. I knew because I had visited him on a couple of occasions in the early days of the war just after setting up as a private detective.

Then the terrible implication struck me. My God, I thought, the fiend was taking David home. He must be holding Sheila prisoner there. As this notion came to me as frighteningly fast and violent as a lightning flash, I felt both excited and horrified in equal measure.

It was then that my natural instincts took over from my brain and within seconds I found myself running – running as if all the devils in hell were on my trail. The neat suburban houses of Sycamore Rise swept past me in a blur as I raced along the pavement heading for Chestnut Avenue, my feet pounding hard on the flagstones. Inconsequently, I chided myself for being so unfit. Fags and booze had certainly taken a toll on my fitness. Nevertheless,

I increased my speed, sweat drenching my shirt and my heart fighting to burst free of my chest. I ran that evening as I have never run in my life before.

At least now I knew where I was going. What I would find when I got there I did not know, but the thought filled me with dread.

THIRTY-SIX

The boot was empty. Northcote leaned forward and saw the gaping, damaged partition – his prisoner's escape route.

'You won't find me in there,' said a voice behind him.

David had not expected Northcote to react with such speed and violence. He had thought that the shock of finding the boot empty would have confused his captor and therefore slowed his reactions.

But this was not the case.

Swiftly and with a nimbleness that belied his size, Northcote swung round on the balls of his feet with great alacrity and lunged at David with the knife. To his dismay, David was the one who was caught by surprise and although he pulled back swiftly and dodged sideways in an attempt to avoid the sharp blade, he was not quick enough to go beyond Northcote's reach. The knife pierced his shoulder, the blade going in deep. David felt a searing hot pain and he dropped to his knees, his vision blurring. Suddenly he was aware that his mouth was filled with vomit and before he could expel it, he collapsed unconscious on the gravel drive.

Northcote stood over him, legs apart like a grisly colossus and laughed.

* * *

When David recovered consciousness, the first thing that he became aware of was the searing pain in his shoulder. Gradually as his vision and memory asserted themselves, he became aware that he was in his own kitchen. He was sitting facing the table on which lay the body of his wife, Sheila. She was dressed only in her brassière and knickers and had tape across her mouth. She wasn't moving but it was clear from the rise of her chest that she was alive.

David made to go to her. It was only then he realised that he was bound tightly to the chair.

'Just sit where you are. Don't try to move, Inspector. I've had enough trouble with you already.'

The voice came from behind him. It was Northcote.

'I've arranged a ringside seat for you, Inspector,' said Northcote, moving round to face him.

'You swine, let me go.' David knew that his words were impotent. The man was cruel and he was mad. Nothing but a bullet through the heart would stop him now.

'Let me explain what I intend to do so that the anticipation of the event will bring you as much anguish, discomfort and pain as possible. Almost as much as the event itself. But I can assure you that it will be spectacularly upsetting. You see, I really want to make you suffer, really suffer. It is because of you I festered away in a little white cell for eight years – eight long years. Have you any concept what that is like? To wake up each morning knowing that you will be staring at the same blank four walls for the rest of the day. There will be no one to talk to or be with. The same – day after day after day. That is your life, if you can call it life. There is no one to talk with. No one to share things with. There is just nothing. The brain atrophies and the bitterness grows. It festers, Inspector and becomes focused. It focused on you – because it was you who gave me that fate and indeed nothing I can do to you can possibly make up for the pain and distress I suffered. They say that revenge is a dish best served up cold. Well, Inspector, this one is going to be particularly icy.'

Northcote chuckled at his own conceit and walked over to a kitchen cabinet near the sink. Here rested an instrument case which he opened and extracted a long shiny scalpel. He ran it gently across face of his thumb causing fine line of scarlet to appear. He sucked it noisily.

He grinned. 'Nice and sharp. A very efficient slicing tool.'

'What are you going to do?' David could hardly make his mouth work and these words emerged almost as a hoarse whisper.

'I am so glad you asked me that. Fear not, it is my intention to explain everything to you in great detail.'

Holding the scalpel aloft, he moved to the kitchen table and stood over the inert form of Sheila Llewellyn. For a moment he looked down at her, lost in dark thoughts his eyes lit with a wild fire and then after a moment he broke his gaze and turned to David.

'Lovely smooth arms your wife has got, Inspector. And that is where I intend to start.'

David's stomach lurched and he groaned. 'Please, I beg you, leave her be. Use me, cut me instead. I'm the one you hate. She hasn't done you any harm. Please leave her alone.'

'Oh, yes, you are the one I hate and indeed I will come to you in due course, Inspector. But here's the beauty of all this. In cutting up your wife, I manage to hurt you twice. As she suffers, so will you. As she screams, so will you. A wonderful chorus of pain and despair, And I haven't even started on you yet. There's a beautiful symmetry about it all.'

David's head slumped down in abject despair.

'Come, come, Inspector. You have a ringside seat. I expect you to watch. You see I will begin slowly by taking a pleasing slice of flesh from the upper arm – not too deep, not as deep as the bone, but deep enough to provide a tasty piece of meat about the size of a rump steak. A little appetiser before the main feast. Internal organs are the best for that particular course.'

David swore loudly and with all his might he tried to move, to break free of his bonds, but it was to no avail. The more he tugged and wriggled, the tighter his bonds appeared to grow.

'Once I have secured our lovely slice of arm, so welcome in these days of meat rationing, I do not intend to be selfish. I will devour half and allow you to snack on the rest. Oh, do not look so revolted. I shall insist that you share the tasty morsel. Refusal to do so will mean more pain for your wife. So you see in a way by tasting her flesh you will be doing her a favour.'

'You bastard!' David bellowed at the top of his voice, the words echoing dully around the kitchen.

Northcote just beamed. 'Indubitably, I am a bastard. Oh, yes. But a clever one. You've got to give me that. A clever bastard who has the upper hand. Now, I think it is time I begin.'

He leaned over Sheila Llewellyn and with a steady motion brought the scalpel down towards her bare arm.

THIRTY-SEVEN

By the time I reached Larch Close, my lungs were on the verge of bursting. I imagined them, barrage balloon-like inflating beyond their accepted capacity inside my aching chest surging up towards my mouth. Surely they would burst at any time? But until they did, I kept on running. Two people's lives could depend on me. I just hoped that fate would be kind and allow me to arrive in time to prevent the terrible scenario my mind had conjured up.

At last I reached David's house. I skidded as I turned down past the gateway and moderated my speed. I spied the car that Northcote had been driving parked by the side of the neat villa at the end of the tree-lined drive. There were lights on in the downstairs rooms and I discovered that the front door was unlocked.

It had been two or three years since I had been in the house so that my memory of its geography was a little hazy. I stood in the hallway and listened. I was still breathing heavily from my exertions and my own breath, for a time, masked any other noises in the house. Desperately, I tried to control my breathing and as I succeeded, I heard voices or to be precise one voice. It was muffled and indistinct. There was no way that I could identify it or tell what it was saying. However I could deduce that it was male.

I opened the door of the sitting room. It was empty, but I could now detect that the noise I could hear was coming from the kitchen beyond, the door of which was closed. I crossed the room at speed. I knew that this wasn't the time to eavesdrop. Seconds were precious, especially when there was a madman involved. I also thought that a surreptitious opening of the door would be more dangerous than slamming it open. This way, whatever was going on in that room would for a few moments stop, freeze, as it were, and all attention would be on me.

Clasping my gun in one hand, I placed my other on the door handle. As I did so, a high pitched scream rent the air. I slammed the door open and rushed into the room. As quickly as I could in that moment of startled silence I tried to take in the scene before me. To my right, I saw David, pale and drawn, bound to a heavy dining chair, his eyes wide with panic. In the centre of the room, on a kitchen table lay the body of a barely clad woman whom I dimly recognised as Sheila Llewellyn. Standing over her with what looked like a small vicious knife was Dr Ralph Northcote. He had just made a cut in Sheila's arm, a thin trickle of blood ran down onto the table top.

On seeing me, the madman glared at me with wild animal ferocity and with a roar of rage took a step in my direction. I fired my gun. I did not have time to aim accurately and the bullet whizzed past the devil. He lunged at me. I fired again. This time my aim was surer. It caught him in his right arm. He gave a cry of pain but this did not stop him. Before I knew it, he was on me.

We crashed to the floor, the gun slipped from my grasp. The power and weight of my assailant pinned me down to the ground. He growled and slobbered like a giant bear over me. I couldn't reach my gun so I punched him as hard as I could in the face but that did not deter the devil either. He seemed to be functioning on some kind of obsessive energy that ignored pain. He raised the knife high above his head ready to plunge it in me. I struggled to break free but failed to extricate myself completely. As I slithered sideways, he stabbed me in the shoulder. In an instant, despite the excruciating pain my hands sought out his throat and squeezed hard against the thick flesh. Still the monster was not deterred. He raised the knife again.

Then there was a shot. It sounded like a thunderclap in my ear.

Northcote grimaced and his body froze. The blade only inches away from my face – from my good eye!

As he faltered, I pulled myself from under him and rolled aside on the floor out of his range. Then I saw blood suddenly fountain from his throat. It frothed and bubbled around his Adam's apple. He had been shot in the back of the neck. With an obscene gurgle, he fell face downwards on the floor where seconds earlier I had been lying.

I gazed up and saw Sheila Llewellyn. Her face was ashen and haunted, her eyes wide and blank as though she were in some kind of hypnotic trance. She was standing by the kitchen table, one arm resting on it for support. In the other hand she held my gun. Fine tendrils of smoke were still emerging from its muzzle.

THIRTY-EIGHT

'Well, boyo, this is a turn up for the book,' observed my friend David Llewellyn without a trace of irony. 'I never expected to wind up in a hospital bed next to you. And we're both suffering from the same complaint: a wound to the shoulder.'

'Life is funny that way,' I mused.

It was the morning following the night before. The horrendous night before when I had tackled Ralph Northcote and Sheila Llewellyn had shot the demon in the back of the neck, killing him. In the end, apart from being terribly shaken and no doubt the inheritor of ghastly nightmares for some months to come, Sheila was the least physically damaged of the three of us. Luckily, Northcote had only just begun his butchering work and the scalpel had only broken the skin. She had just a nasty little cut on her upper arm. However, David and I had both been badly wounded in the shoulder by Northcote's scalpel: almost an identical twin branding, as though we were initiates into a very brutal and bloody secret society.

After the police had arrived and taken Northcote's corpse off to the morgue at Scotland Yard, we had been scooped up by ambulance and taken to Charing Cross Hospital for treatment and an overnight stay. The injuries were not life threatening just painful and inconvenient. At least we were alive, as David had reminded me on more that one occasion. He had revived both in energy and outlook with remarkable resilience and as the morning light streamed through the windows of the small ward in which we were incarcerated, he seemed to have metamorphosed back into his old cheerful self. I suppose the fact that Sheila was alive and no longer in danger and that Northcote was on a slab in the police morgue had a lot to do with his revived demeanour. His nightmare had evaporated. I was delighted for him.

The door opened and a pretty nurse entered carrying a tray with two mugs of tea and two plates of biscuits.'

'Our elevenses, eh, nurse? I could get used to this pampering,' said David brightly.

The girl smiled. 'I don't think you're going to get a chance. Once the doctor's has a look at you, I reckon he'll be sending you home. You'll just need to take it easy for a few weeks and you'll both be as right as ninepence."

'That's a shame. I was counting on a long stay in here,' grinned David.

After the nurse departed, we drank our tea in silence. I could not get the images of the events of the previous night from my mind: my race along the darkening streets; my dramatic entrance into the kitchen and the dreadful sight that greeted me; my desperate tussle with Northcote; the shot and the terrible frothing wound at his throat. I shuddered as these dramatic pictures flickered before me as though they were projected on a screen. I looked across at David and could see from his furrowed brow and staring eyes that he too was experiencing his own private horror show. At least his loved-one was safe and sound. If only I could have done the same for my sweet Max. If only I could have saved her. With a determined effort I shut down that avenue of thought. That way madness lies.

The door opened again and three individuals bustled in. We had visitors: Sheila, Benny and Peter.

'We've come to see the heroes,' chimed Benny.

'Survivors more like,' grinned David as Sheila embraced him and then planted a large kiss on his cheek.

'I'd hug you, my darling, but I'm afraid my arm isn't up

to it yet,' she said.

'I can wait,' said David, returning the kiss.

She stroked her husband's face affectionately. Although her face was pale and she looked tired, Sheila seemed remarkably robust for a lady who had undergone such a terrible ordeal less than twenty-four hours earlier.

'In the wars again, eh, Johnny,' said Benny, pulling up a chair by my bed.

'I'll do anything for a cup of tea in bed and being fussed over by a pretty nurse.'

'You know, one of these days, I'll be coming to the morgue to identify your body, Johnny Hawke.'

'More than likely.'

'You need more protection,' piped up Peter. 'An assistant to help you. To watch your back.'

'An assistant like you, you mean.'

Peter's eyes brightened. 'Exactly. I could leave school this summer and come and work for you.'

'I don't make enough money to keep myself from teetering towards the breadline, let alone support an assistant.'

'But with the two of us, we could double the business.'

'You wouldn't let him, would you Johnny? He's too young to be involved in your nasty line of work.'

'I'm already involved,' asserted Peter. 'I helped Johnny catch Bruce Horsefield. He couldn't have done it without me.'

'It's madness,' moaned Benny.

I agreed with him, but I also knew of Peter's one-track determination. I wasn't sure whether it would be wise to take him in under my umbrella rather than risk him doing something foolish and trying out on his own. He was headstrong enough to do that. Whatever, now was not the time or place to consider such possibilities.

Thankfully, Benny read my mind and changed the subject. 'When will you be going home?'

'Today, I hope.'

'Today! But you are seriously injured.'

I grinned. 'I've got a very nasty cut, that's all. It's deep and painful but no damage has been done, although I'll never play the violin again.'

'Really… I never knew… Ah, a joke.' He smiled with that strange disapproving grin that was peculiar to him.

* * *

Some hours later, I was standing in the room alone. We, the fellow members of the damaged shoulder club had both been discharged with appointments in the outpatients in seven days' time. David had been whisked off by Sheila, who had given me a gentle hug, while whispering the words, 'Thank you,' in my ear.

My arm was in a neat sling and the nurse had very kindly draped my jacket and overcoat over my shoulders like a cloak before hurrying off for more important duties. Well, there was a war on.

I needed a smoke. Some stimulation before I faced the outside world once more. A smoke was such a normal comforting thing. But now it wasn't going to be easy to organise. I sat on the bed and with great difficulty extracted a cigarette from my jacket pocket and slipped it in my mouth. Now, I thought, how on earth am I going to light the beggar, when a match flared near me and was held close to the end of my cigarette.

I looked up at my helpmate and gazed into the face of Ivana. She smiled.

'Light it quickly, or I'll get my fingers burned.'

I obeyed, inhaling the smoke with gusto.

'Benny told me you were here. You have a habit of ending up on hospital beds.'

'It's my only opportunity to meet pretty women.'

Her eyes twinkled with amusement and then darkened suddenly. 'You don't mind me coming here, do you?' she said hesitantly.

'Mind! Of course not. You are a gorgeous sight for this sore eye.' I leaned forward and kissed her on the cheek.

'In that case, Mr Hawke, I suggest that I take you home and cook you a very nice meal to help build up your strength. What do you say?'

Sparkling Books

Young adult fiction

Cheryl Bentley, *Petronella & The Trogot*
Brian Conaghan, *The Boy Who Made it Rain*
Luke Hollands, *Peregrine Harker and The Black Death*

Crime: mystery, thriller, horror fiction

Thomas Brown, *Lynnwood*
Nikki Dudley, *Ellipsis*
Sally Spedding, *Cold Remains*
Sally Spedding, *Malediction*

Other fiction

Anna Cuffaro, *Gatwick Bear and the Secret Plans*
Amanda Sington-Williams, *The Eloquence of Desire*

Non-fiction

Daniele Cuffaro, *American Myths in Post-9/11 Music*
David Kauders, *The Greatest Crash: How contradictory policies are sinking the global economy*

Revivals

Gustave Le Bon, *Psychology of Crowds*

For more information visit:
www.sparklingbooks.com

Sparkling Books